THE ANIMAL RESCUE AGENCY

400

Case File: Little Claws

THE ANIMAL RESCUE AGENCY

Case File: Little Claws

BY **ELIOT SCHREFER**

ILLUSTRATED BY
DANIEL DUNCAN

KATHERINE TEGEN BOOKS
An Imprint of HarperCollins Publishers

For Eric

PROLOGUE

Little Claws yawned and opened his eyes for the first time in months. What woke him up?

A dripping sound.

Snow melting into the den.

Springtime!

He leaped into the air, landing right on his mother's face. She grunted, batted him to one side, and placed her large white paws over her eyes. "It's not time yet. Go back to sleep."

Little Claws bit into her ear and tugged. "I know what spring sounds like! Now we go outside!"

"No, no," his mother, Big Claws, grumbled. "We're going to sleep for a long time more."

"You can if you want. *I'm* going outside." This was his second spring awakening, and he knew how it worked. He leaped up and clawed at the snow. Bits of sleet fell into the den.

"Little Claws . . . ," Big Claws warned.

But it was too late. A circle of sunlight had appeared in the roof, and chill air streamed in. Little Claws took a deep sniff. He smelled seawater, tender young bird, salty arctic fish. He bounded out of the den.

Big Claws groaned. Am I the only mother who lets her cub get away with this sort of thing? she thought.

"Come on!" Little Claws called from outside.

Big Claws knew that her cub could be in danger from male polar bears. She'd better get out there and protect him. Grumbling, she lifted herself up to sitting and stretched her long-unused limbs. Whether she was ready for it or not, spring was here.

"It's amazing out, Mom!" Little Claws called.

Big Claws poked her head out of the den, shaking sleep from her eyes. She saw a long expanse of unbroken ice, deeper and smoother and cleaner than when they'd bedded down at the beginning of winter.

But where was her cub? She called for Little Claws, sniffed the air worriedly.

Something whizzed toward her. She jerked, turning just in time to get struck full in the snout by a snowball.

"Happy spring, Mom!" Little Claws called, popping up from behind a snowdrift. "Your turn! Try and get me!"

"Do not throw a snowball at your mother. Ever again," she growled.

A second snowball hit her, this one glancing off the top of her head and spraying into crystals. Little Claws stared at her, mouth wide open in glee, waiting for her to react.

Snarling, Big Claws stood on her two back paws.

Little Claws shrank in fear. Maybe he had gone too far.

Big Claws turned away for a moment, as if to get her anger under control, then slowly faced her son again. Only now she had a big snowball in her paws. It was as big as Little Claws himself.

His eyes widened. "Mom? No. You wouldn't."

"Oh yes I would." And she did. Soon he was covered, nose to tail, in powdery snow.

"Ah-ha!" he said, pouncing through the snow piles. "Good one! I'll get you back for that!"

Laughing, his mother tailed him through the drifts, dodging his snowballs as best she could and getting off a few of her own. Soon their stomachs would be rumbling, but for now there was no harm in having some fun.

She charged Little Claws, growling. Giggling, he bounded away, somersaulting down a snowy slope. He became a ball of white fur, gaining more and more speed as he went.

Down at the bottom was a stretch of ice, and then the frigid sea. The water looked gray and cold, but it would be no real danger if Little Claws fell in—he had thick fur to keep the chill away. Though he hadn't really learned to swim, he could paddle a few feet back to shore with no problem.

It was something else that made Big Claws's heart seize. Standing at the horizon was a dark figure, totally still. And Little Claws was rocketing toward it.

Little Claws belly flopped onto the ice at the bottom of the hill, giggling. "Get down here, Mom! That was so great!"

She stood up on her back legs and stared at the figure. It looked like a man. She'd seen them on the decks of ships, but humans were never on foot this far north. This was a land of animals only. Big Claws wanted to cry out to her cub, but didn't want to attract the stranger's attention. She started down the slope.

Little Claws didn't seem to notice the human. He was busy plowing through fluffy snow, making tunnels and sprays of powdery white.

The figure held still, making no move to approach. It was definitely a human. A tall one, Big Claws could see now that she was closer. And here was the strange thing: he was wearing a hat made of white fur. She'd never seen such a thing.

It was the color of polar bear fur.

Still unaware, Little Claws was tumbling and playing. He sprinted toward the water, sending a flock of arctic birds squawking into the air. When they landed, he took off after them again.

He was moving farther and farther away from Big Claws.

She bounded down the slope, toward her son. The snow gave under her, and she started plowing down. It was all she could do to stay right-side up as she went.

As she reached the bottom, the arctic birds took off over open water. Little Claws turned and watched her. "Did you see? I almost caught one, Mom!"

"Come back!" Big Claws ordered, sprinting across the ice. She noticed something strange separating her from Little Claws. A black line. Not a crack, but something laid on top of the ice. It led to a device the man in the white fur hat had down by his feet.

"Are you worried the ice will break?" Little Claws called. He hopped into the air and back down on the frozen ground, sending seawater sloshing over the sides. "Because I checked it, just like you taught me to. It'll hold me!"

Big Claws tossed her head in the direction of the man in the white fur hat. "We're not alone."

"Really?" Little Claws said, tottering on his back

legs as he peered around. "I don't see anyone."

"It's because you're too small," Big Claws said as she continued toward her son. "But you'll just have to trust—"

The man in the white fur hat leaned over his device, and then there was a distant click. The dark line that had been laid on top of the ice roared and burst into light. The air boomed, snow and ice spraying up all around Big Claws. She shielded her eyes and managed to stay upright under the blast. When she uncovered her face, she saw that the explosion had kicked so much frost into the air that she couldn't see more than a few feet in front of her.

She roared and lunged to her cub despite the ice spray that still clogged the air, that stung her nose and bit her lungs.

When enough of the air had cleared, she could finally see what had happened to Little Claws. She pulled up short and groaned.

He'd been knocked to the ground by the blast. He struggled to get to his paws, his eyes wide with fear. "Mom!"

The man's explosion had caused a giant crevasse to appear between the two of them. It was widening in front of her eyes.

Little Claws was heading out to sea.

He was in the middle of his ice floe, limbs splayed out and claws digging in as he desperately tried to keep his balance in the rough waves. "Help me!" he shrieked.

"I'm coming!" she said. Her little one hadn't practiced swimming yet—teaching him how was one of the first activities she'd planned for this spring. She'd have to swim to him, not the other way around. He dug his claws into the ice, his body sweeping from side to side as the waves rocked the floe. Big Claws leaped into the water, sending up more giant waves. She snorted as frigid seawater entered her nose and stung her eyes.

She swam toward Little Claws, her gaze trained on her cub. She was a powerful swimmer and cut a smooth course through the waves. But the arctic currents were strong. Every time she came to the crest of a wave and got a view of the floe, it—and Little Claws—was farther away.

Her son was disappearing.

As the sea pulled him farther out, his voice got weaker. "Help me, Mom!" he called.

Big Claws kept up her swimming speed despite the

burning feeling deep in her muscles. She'd sooner die than let her son disappear. But as the floe sped away into the open sea, she had to make a decision. She could chase after it, and likely drown, or return to solid land and try to find another way.

"I'll rescue you, I promise!" she called after her son. "Just hold tight, my love!"

Heart heaving, she turned around and paddled toward shore.

Exhausted, she dragged herself back onto solid ice. What could she possibly do to rescue Little Claws?

As she panted, coughing out seawater and sucking in air, she recovered enough to see that the man in the white hat was still on the horizon. He was staring out to sea, precisely where her cub was trapped on his floe.

He'd done this to them. But why?

She was tempted to sprint toward the man, to punish him for what he'd done. But she was tired, and her first priority was Little Claws. He hadn't had a bite to eat since he came out of hibernation, and here he was, trapped at sea. If he didn't get rescued within a few days, he'd starve. And that was only part of the danger: If he fell into the water, he'd drown. If he drifted far enough south that the ice melted, he'd drown.

But Big Claws had no way to get out to sea. She knew she couldn't rescue her son on her own.

She needed help.

And when an animal truly needed help, there was only one place to turn.

The Animal Rescue Agency.

Artist rendering of incident off the coast of TernPolarBearWalrusCalves. Please relay to Esquire Fox of the Animal Rescue Agency A.S.A.P. URGENT.

"What is this a picture of?" Esquire asked, tapping her claw on the computer screen.

"Don't do that. You'll break it!" Mr. Pepper said crossly. "Computers are expensive, and they're not designed for foxes."

"Strong words from someone who pecks all day," Esquire said. They'd been trading jabs about claws and beaks for years. The fox's good antique table had pockmarks up and down its legs from whenever Mr. Pepper pecked it by accident while he was doing housework.

With a burst of his wings, the rooster hopped to the arm of Esquire's desk chair, so he could see the screen better. "It's obvious what that is, you numbskull of a fox. It's perfectly clear that it's a . . . a . . ."

". . . perfectly clear that it's a . . . ?" Esquire prompted.

"Why, it's . . . a hippopotamus being abducted by a space amoeba!"

"I'm sorry, what did you just say?" Esquire asked, tilting her head to the side. She toyed with her whiskers in an attempt to hide the smile that played on her lips. "Oh yes. Now I see. That's quite obviously a hippo being abducted by a space amoeba. Thank you for your insight, Mr. Pepper."

"Happy to oblige," Mr. Pepper said, hopping to the rug and returning to his dusting. "Now, kindly remove your paws from the coffee table."

Esquire kept her paws where they were and flicked her tail as she scrutinized the image. Though she'd said so to Mr. Pepper, she very much doubted that this was a hippopotamus being abducted by a space amoeba. Especially not one in the Arctic, which is what animals meant by the phrase "TernPolarBearWalrusCalves." The North Pole would be a very unusual place for a hippopotamus. (Or a space amoeba, for that matter.)

Esquire's Animal Rescue Agency had a network of operatives around the world, and they were good at their jobs—but she couldn't help an animal in distress until she'd heard about it! Since most creatures were too small to travel very far in one go, they relayed word, beast by beast and bird by bird, down the globe until it got to Esquire Fox. The original artist's rendering might have been given to a hare, who relayed it to a puffin, who got it to an albatross, who flew to the mainland and described it to a wolf, who ran it with her pack until they found an elk who drew it in the dirt with his antlers, so moles could sense the vibration of the picture and redraw it, then transmit it through their underground tunnels to the roaches in the local library, who logged in after hours to email their rendition to the Animal Rescue Agency, where a blinking alarm light notified Esquire of the incoming message. There was a lot of room for an artist's rendering to change over the course of all that. To be perfectly honest, roaches weren't good artists even in the best of circumstances.

Esquire leaned her narrow foxy head close to the screen, so close that it tickled her whiskers. The stranded hippopotamus, or whatever this creature actually was, looked very worried. That fact plus a rough location was enough to get her started.

"I'm going to take the six-fifteen train north, Mr. Pepper!" Esquire called. She closed the computer window and stood, dusting her paws on her waistcoat. "Where's my suitcase? The nice new one from Senegal, with the brass fasteners?"

Mr. Pepper appeared in the kitchen entranceway, feather duster clamped in his beak. He managed to speak around it. "You're not really setting off to fight a space amoeba, are you?"

"Well, that's the thing," Esquire said, tugging on her soft leather moccasins. She wore them only on her back paws, like she was a person. "I'm not totally convinced that this is a space amoeba, Mr. Pepper."

"I don't see what else it could be," Mr. Pepper huffed. "But I suppose that hippo is in trouble, and we can't go closing our eyes to an animal in trouble. We'll take the evening train together."

"I'm afraid you won't be coming on this mission," Esquire said. "There will be plenty of wolves and polar bears. Even if you avoid becoming someone's lunch, it will be far too cold. The Arctic Circle is no place for a chicken."

Most animals had the irritatingly primitive habit of naming regions by the types of animals that lived there. TernPolarBearWalrusCalves would be very far north indeed—in the iciest regions of the North Pole. As a fox, Esquire could count on her fur thickening as she went north, but Mr. Pepper's feathers wouldn't do the same.

"What do you mean, I won't be coming?" Mr. Pepper clucked, dropping the duster in indignation. "I always come! Do you think I'm going to let you lose your tail to a hunter? Who will make sure you eat proper meals? Who's going to see that you remember to collect payment? Of course I'm coming. Indeed!" He continued his outraged clucking as he levered open a cabinet and dragged out a wicker valise with his beak. It clattered to the tiled floor. "Here's your darned Senegalese suitcase with the brass fasteners."

Esquire Fox considered resisting, but to date she'd never won an open argument with Mr. Pepper. Once he'd decided on a course of action, he simply couldn't be swayed. Even now he was pacing the room angrily, muttering "some foxes!" over and over to himself.

It was a strange life, Esquire knew, a fox sharing a home with an old rooster. But she and Mr. Pepper had been working together for years. And Esquire was no normal fox.

It was a very nice home, and Esquire would be sorry to be away from it for this mission. Her delicately carved rock walls displayed art she'd collected from around the world. The floor was covered in rugs, the largest one woven in the Himalayas by the sheep themselves as a thank-you after Esquire had saved them from an avalanche. Mr. Pepper made sure the rugs were perfectly clean each morning, picking out any bits of dirt with his beak. Esquire Fox hadn't grown up in a home nearly as nice as this one. Even as a little kit she'd thought her family's den was a terrible place, cluttered with dirt and duck bones and reeking of pee. It had been her life's work to set up this civilized headquarters for a legitimate global organization. The agency had started with her very first rescue—Mr. Pepper himself.

Now she had an important concern: What to wear to the Arctic? It wouldn't do to arrive looking unprepared. She'd definitely bring her creamy woolen scarf, which would set off her orange fur nicely and serve as camouflage on snowfields. And the boots with the soft lining—of course she'd need those!

As she neatly folded her flannel shirts and laid them in the suitcase, Esquire heard clucking beside her and watched as Mr. Pepper dropped in a pair of chicken-scale earmuffs. They were actually cotton balls glued to a rubber band, but neither of them talked about that. Chicken ears are covered by feathers anyway, so it didn't much matter what Mr. Pepper decided to consider earmuffs.

"Mr. Pepper, I really don't think you should—" Esquire started.

"I won't hear it. There is no way that you are doing this alone," Mr. Pepper said. "Get moving, the evening train will be here before we know it."

Esquire had chosen this location for the Animal Rescue Agency's secret headquarters precisely because it was only a few hundred feet from a rail line that humans used to ship freight. If she and Mr. Pepper jumped onto that evening's train, they could switch to a ship in Seattle, followed by another train that would bring them into Anchorage by the same time the next day. Then she'd mobilize her chain of operatives to get them as far north as they could go. "If you're coming, you'll need more than earmuffs." Esquire sighed. "Where's your coat?"

To the suitcase she added her new woolen gloves, the ones a friendly ewe from the local farm had given as payment. They had the tips snipped off so she could hold lockpicks in her pawtips. Mr. Pepper dropped in his heavy coat, which was actually a quilted teapot cozy with the top cut off so he could pop his head through.

Esquire could wear clothes made for the smallest human children, but Mr. Pepper was a bantam rooster, which meant he barely came up to Esquire's knee. He was never without his lacy apron, frilled up the sides with strawberries embroidered on the front. Much as Mr. Pepper irritated her, Esquire would be beside herself if the day ever came when she couldn't look up from her book and see him fussing about her lair in his strawberry apron.

"So," Mr. Pepper said. "How much does this hippopotamus offer as a fee?"

Esquire went totally still.

So did Mr. Pepper. Then his feathers fluffed until he was twice the size he was a moment ago. That was never a good sign. "You are charging, right?" he asked, his voice rising to a dangerous squawk. "You do realize that's how businesses work, right?"

Mr. Pepper was always getting on Esquire to request some sort of payment from each of their rescue targets. Wool, seeds, handicrafts, that sort of thing. "I figured I'd settle the terms once I arrived. Like a gentlefox does. No need to iron everything out right away, you know."

"There is not enough billing coming in!" Mr. Pepper shrilled. "We cannot run a business without billing!"

Esquire closed her eyes against Mr. Pepper's onslaught, only opening them once he'd gone quiet. When she did, she saw that he was delicately using his beak to transfer woolen socks from her drawer to her traveling case, one by one. "Thank you for the help, Mr. Pepper," Esquire said with a wink.

"I can't even imagine the trouble you'd get into without me," he huffed. "I shudder at the very thought of it!"

Esquire's eyes went to the rescue agency's console, where a light was blinking. This was going to be a high-stakes job—trouble was the one thing guaranteed to be on the agenda.

INCOMING ANIMAL
DISTRESS CALLS

EXTRA URGENT

Agency Operatives

CHAPTER

Esquire thought she'd been cold a few minutes ago. But that was before they'd reached the mountain's peak. Wind sheared up from the cliffs below like a blade, jabbing between the fibers of her tweed and under her lined hood. It had taken a lot of convincing, but a shivering Mr. Pepper had finally allowed himself to be tucked into Esquire's jacket. Even so, he was trembling against her, his eyes scrunched tight against the cold.

The husky stood facing them, patiently awaiting directions.

Esquire gave the dogsled a light kick. "You're absolutely sure this thing is sturdy?"

The husky arf-ed and pranced, the snowballs that were clumping her fur shaking and jangling. She spoke with the thick accent of the local dogs, and Esquire hadn't understood a word she'd yet said.

In the distance below were the winking lights of Utqiagvik, the northernmost city in the United States. The last stop for civilization. Or human civilization, at least. This far north, the weak springtime sun stayed up for only a few hours before going back down, which meant they had to hustle if they wanted to be indoors before night fell.

"So you want us to . . . get in this?" Esquire asked, tapping a claw against the rim of the dogsled. Well, *dogsled*—it still had the insignia of a dairy on its side. Humans would call it a milk crate.

"Get a move on!" Mr. Pepper clucked from deep within Esquire's tweed jacket. "It'll be dark soon, and you'll still be yammering and stalling up here on the mountaintop."

"Arf!" the husky agreed.

Esquire took a moment to pluck stray twigs and leaves from inside the milk crate, using her handkerchief to wipe the bottom as clean as she could. Then she folded herself inside and gave her head a good shake to free her ears of snow. "Okay, mush!" she said.

Supposedly that was what one said to sled dogs, and she'd wanted to try it for some time.

The husky surged into action—by leaping right off the cliff face. For a moment the milk-crate sled was still, and Esquire watched in horror as the dog disappeared off the mountaintop, a slick of slightly melted snow the only remaining sign of her. Esquire placed her nose under her lapel so Mr. Pepper could hear her. "Get rea—!"

The lead connecting the crate to the sled dog snapped taut, and suddenly they were catapulted through the air. Esquire yelled out despite herself, pressing all four limbs into the corners of the crate so she and Mr. Pepper didn't hurtle out into the frigid sky.

After a heart-dropping moment of free fall, the crate sled slammed into the ground below, sending up plumes of powder. The husky looked back to check on them, joyously barked, and then they were in motion again, plowing through the snow. It geysered away on either side as they raced toward the town. Now that she wasn't free-falling anymore, Esquire enjoyed the experience. They were surrounded by walls of white, the stars winking to life in the twilight sky above. "You have to pop your head out and see this, Mr. Pepper!" Esquire called into her jacket.

"I'll do no such fool thing," he clucked, his words only barely audible through Esquire's tweed. "My coxcomb would freeze off!"

"Well, it's your loss—whoa!" Esquire covered her head with her paws as the sled slalomed directly for a snowcapped boulder. But the husky turned at the last minute, sending the crate skating over the ice in a broad arc. Only by perching her body high on one edge was Esquire able to keep it from flipping over. "Excuse me, Madame Husky, but maybe you don't need to go *quite* so fast," she called. But the dog didn't seem to listen— or maybe all she heard was the equivalent of "mush!" because she started going faster.

"What is going *on* out there?" came Mr. Pepper's muffled voice.

"Hold on tight!"

After the husky checked to make sure no human cars were driving past, she bounded onto a roadway, the ground turning icier beneath the sled as they crossed a bridge. They were nearly in civilization now. From between the husky's flapping ears, Esquire could see the yellow perimeter lights of snow-locked Utqiagvik. Before long, they were on the town's lonely streets. It looked just like the landscape outside town, since the asphalt was hidden far below snow and ice. Most of the doors were shuttered, lights glowing inside as the residents settled in for the night.

The husky brought them to a quiet intersection, where Esquire could tell from the intact snow that no people or cars had passed in a long time. Esquire got out with Mr. Pepper. The dog nodded once, then raced out of town.

"Thank you, see you in the morning!" Esquire called after the husky, watching her fluffy tail wag cheerfully as she sped away. They'd agreed that the dog would leave as soon as she delivered them, and they'd all meet up later at their camp outside town. The dog was in the business of transporting animals, not people, and if she didn't want to be captured by a human kennel master, it was best she spent as little time as possible in civilization.

Esquire let out a long breath, sending vapor freezing and sparkling into the fading light. Utqiagvik was a grim, desolate place. Her heart told her she ought to do like the husky and get Mr. Pepper and herself out of there as soon as possible. They would do precisely that, soon enough—but first they had to see what information they could gather in town. She rubbed her gloved paws together. Maybe they could warm themselves up while they were at it.

"Left at the fishmonger, then right at the gasoline station," Mr. Pepper instructed from within Esquire's jacket. He was always better at remembering directions. Esquire picked her way along the snowy street, prepared to duck behind a drift the moment she detected any sign of humans. She didn't need the publicity that would follow a human sighting a fox in a tweed waistcoat. If that happened, the Animal Rescue Agency, which relied so much on secrecy, would be ruined. Mr. Pepper was always trying to get her to wear better camouflage. But that would mean looking not nearly as snazzy. Besides, it was close enough to sundown that all the local humans appeared to be in for the night.

"Left at the fishmonger . . . and now right at the gasoline station!" she said to herself as she went. They'd gotten directions from her nearest regional operative, a moose headquartered in Anchorage, whom she'd once rescued after he got his antlers tangled in power lines. His directions had been a bit fuzzy, because he'd never actually *been* to Utqiagvik. One of Mr. Pepper's goals was to recruit them a proper arctic operative while they were on this mission. "We're almost there," Esquire whispered to Mr. Pepper.

Soon enough, she came upon the twinkling lights of a pub. Humans sat in the windows, carousing and singing, flagons of warming liquids in their hands. It looked appealing enough, full of cheer and the ruddy light of a roaring fire. But a human pub was nowhere Esquire wanted to be. Her destination was farther down the street. She got down to all fours, pressing her woolen cap tight over her ears. She'd have to pass right by the windows—she hoped these humans would be so absorbed in their revelry that they wouldn't glance outside.

Esquire darted past the first window, then pressed her back against the solid brick wall, making sure no one was looking before she flitted past the next window. Only one more to go.

This time, when Esquire darted forward on all fours, she sensed eyes on her. She risked a glance into the window and saw a human . . . staring right at her. Or *through* her, actually. The man's gaze bored like a drill.

Even though Esquire never lost any speed as she raced across the exposed space, her fox instincts heightened, making time seem to slow as she observed everything about this odd human. He had a long, gray face, a nose with whiskers growing out of it, and dark eyes set deep into his cheeks. And here was the strangest part: he wore a hat made out of pure white fur. Esquire had never seen such a thing.

Actually, there was something even stranger still: right before Esquire passed out of view, a small smile curled the man's lips. He gave a little nod, as if to say *Why hello, there. I've been waiting for you.*

CHAPTER

E squire shivered, and not just from the cold.

Worried that the man in the white fur hat would come out of the pub, she dashed forward on all fours, Mr. Pepper clucking as he jostled within her jacket. After the pub was a mechanic's shop. Its wide rolling door was open, revealing snowmobiles and trucks in various stages of repair, some up high on hydraulic lifts and others lying on their sides on the shop floor.

Esquire risked a moment's pause to do a quick scan of the premises and saw that the two mechanics on duty were turned away, busy welding one of the vehicles. Keeping well clear of the orange sparks cascading from their tools, Esquire ducked into the doorway and skirted the wall. As long as she didn't knock anything over and make a racket, she wasn't worried about being observed. As a general rule, humans tended not to notice the little creatures around them.

In the corner was a loose piece of tile, as Esquire's regional operative had promised. She lifted it and saw a dark open space beneath. Her whiskers just grazed the edges of the hole, so she knew it was wide enough for the rest of her body—that was the purpose of whiskers, after all, to prevent foxes from jumping into burrows that were too small and getting themselves stuck. Esquire hesitated, but the thought of that man in the white fur hat chasing after her goosed her. She plunged into the darkness, nose first.

After a quick scramble, she fell free, instinctively twisting so she landed on all fours. Mr. Pepper tumbled out of her jacket, dropping hackles-down on the floor, skinny chicken legs splayed out in front of him. Esquire's vision filled with orange light, just as cheerful and bright as the human pub's. While she waited for her eyes to adjust, she stood up, dusting off her jacket and fixing her scarf. Mr. Pepper huffed and got to his feet beside her.

"Orders up!" chittered a voice beside her. Esquire

pivoted to let whoever it was pass, and saw a rat bluster-ing by, holding up a tray of steaming drinks.

They were in a narrow space carved out beneath the mechanic's shop, pipes and irregular chunks of con-crete making the floors and walls twist and bulge. A single orange parking light, stolen from a traffic barri-cade and attached to a pilfered battery, shone down on the scene. Clear tubes from the human mechanic's shop ran through the ceiling, the insides bubbling with hot exhaust. They led to big tin casks that humans called mufflers. As Esquire watched, the rat server filled up four bottle caps' worth of hot drink trickling from one of the mufflers, carrying them out to customers on a jar-lid tray. "Orders up, coming through!" he called as he tramped past.

The clientele seemed to be any animal that could fit through the entranceway: Esquire saw mice, rats, snow-white hares, a couple of weasels, a domestic cat, even a pair of beetles staring at each other with roman-tic eyes as they sipped from a bubble of cider on top of a dime. As was the rule among animals, in a communal establishment there might be fighting, sure—but there was no *eating* of one another. That rule got broken once in a while, because urges were urges, but by and large

it could be trusted. Which was why there were mice sitting at a bar, chatting up a cat.

Everyone seemed in good spirits—and why not? Outside it was freezing, but here it was warm. Outside there was danger, but here there was friendship. Outside there were poachers and hunters, but here there were only animals. Esquire picked out a pair of empty stools at the end of the bar, sat on the second to last one, and unbuttoned her tweed jacket. Giving the weasels and cat a nervous side-eye, Mr. Pepper took the last stool. Esquire knew the rooster would prefer to have her between him and anything with sharp teeth. Even when they had the best intentions, carnivores found it hard to restrain themselves when they were around plump old chickens.

The bartender, a rat wearing a greasy stolen mechanic's bandana as an apron, sauntered over. She looked them up and down, rubbing her front paws together. "What'll it be?"

"Whatever hot drink you have fermenting in those mufflers would fit the bill," Esquire said.

"Potato-peel cider tonight," the bartender said. "One coming up!"

Mr. Pepper clucked from his stool.

"Oh, I'm sorry, young man," the bartender said,

leaning over the counter. "Didn't see you down there." She reached under the bar and passed them a cigar box. Esquire placed the box under Mr. Pepper, so he could see over the counter.

"That's much better. Thank you very much," he said.

"Two ciders coming right up," the rat bartender said as she ducked away.

Mr. Pepper fluffed and unfluffed his feathers, flicking away the crystals of ice that had formed underneath, and took a long gander around the rat pub. He'd taken off his teapot cozy, but still looked plenty out of place in his strawberry apron. "Quite a riffraff establishment you've chosen for us," he said.

"You old snob," Esquire chided. "You don't get the inside info about what's happening on the street by going to posh places. We happen to be in a riffraff line of business, Mr. Pepper."

When the rat bartender came back, she had a special twinkle in her eye for Mr. Pepper. "Unusual for us to get a chicken in these parts," she said, leaning over the bar to peer right at him. "At least a chicken that's not cut *into* parts."

Mr. Pepper bristled and opened his mouth to peck. "That is *not* amusing, madame!"

The rat held up her front paws. "Oh, you're a *gentleman*. Sorry to offend." She gave a big wink as she delivered the ciders, placing the two large bottle caps' worth in front of them. "The young master's drink is on the house."

"'Young master,' indeed," Mr. Pepper clucked, head feathers quivering. "How preposterous." But Esquire saw a glimmer in his eye, and suspected he was secretly delighted by that free drink. She laid two linty almonds on the bar as payment for her own cider while Mr. Pepper placed his beak in the bottle cap, pecked and swallowed. He didn't react, but the fact that he wasn't complaining was enough to tell Esquire that he liked it.

"So," Esquire said to the bartender. "You might have realized that we're not from around here."

"Yes," the bartender said. "Most of our local foxes aren't quite as . . . orange. Or wearing jackets."

Esquire stroked her tweed lapel and grinned bashfully. "Rightly so, rightly so." She leaned forward, bringing her voice to a whisper. "In any case, we're here on an urgent mission, with no time to lose. We run the Animal Rescue Agency, you see, and we received a distress call about an animal in dire straits."

"We believe it might be a hippopotamus," Mr. Pepper offered.

"The Animal Rescue Agency!" the rat bartender said loudly. "You don't say. Why, you're famous!"

The rest of the bar went quiet. The fur along the back of Esquire's neck prickled as she realized that everyone was listening, and she cursed as two mice near the entranceway darted upstairs. Esquire and Mr. Pepper were high-profile figures in the animal world, and they'd been betrayed in the past. Some sorts of animals were especially susceptible to bribery—basically, any creature that regularly fell for baited traps was also easily paid off. Lobsters, squirrels, raccoons, and mice were particularly dodgy. Nothing to be done about it now—even if Esquire chased after those mice, there was no way she'd catch them. "Please keep it down," she said through gritted teeth.

"We're honored to have you here," the rat bartender said as the conversations in the room slowly started back up. "But let me tell you something straight. You're here on a fool's errand. The seabird bringing the mother's distress call passed right through here, so I know all about it. That animal you're looking for? He's a *polar bear.*"

Esquire blanched. That did put a wrinkle in things.

"A polar bear would just as soon eat you as look at you," the rat continued. "Even a polar bear cub."

"Yes, I'm well aware of the habits of polar bears," Esquire said. "But our mission is to help any animal who calls us in distress, whatever their position on the food chain. And there's a mother bear out there who's beside herself with worry. When an animal is in danger from humans, all other animals must help. Even if in other circumstances we wouldn't exactly be friends."

The rat bartender shrugged and started wiping glasses. "It's your business, orange fox. What do I know? I'm just a rat."

Esquire turned to address the rest of the bar's patrons. "Do any of you know who might be behind this? Who would intentionally separate a mother polar bear from her cub?"

The animals looked back balefully, then one by one returned to their conversations. All except the domestic cat, who sidled over to the bar. Mr. Pepper played it cool, taking a casual peck-drink of cider, but Esquire noticed his feathers bristle.

"I'm no friend of the polar bears," the cat purred. "I'm not sure any of us are, except for other polar bears. But maybe it's because I have kittens at home that you've touched my heart."

"Do you have a thought?" Esquire asked.

The black cat licked a paw and ran it over her ear,

simultaneously leaning in so she could whisper. Mr. Pepper clucked worriedly as he watched the cat's sharp teeth approach Esquire's ear. "There's a human in town," the cat said. "He comes through this area whenever he's working on his . . . collection. Once he has enough . . . stock, shall we say, he carts it all to the mainland to sell."

"A collection?" Mr. Pepper asked. "What sort of a collection?"

"Well, my delicious rooster . . . it's a collection of *animals*."

Esquire sucked in her breath.

"Why is he collecting animals?" Mr. Pepper asked.

"I have my suspicions," Esquire sighed.

"You should stop this man," the cat said. "We'd all owe a debt to you if you managed it. The truth is that you can't really miss him. He wears this—"

"—white fur hat?" Esquire completed.

The cat flicked her ears, her green eyes widening in surprise. "How did you know that?"

"We . . . looked at each other. It was rather unforgettable."

"Find him and you'll find your polar bear," the black cat said.

"Do you have any idea where he's keeping the

animals he's already collected, or what he plans to do with them?" Esquire asked.

The black cat shook her head. "I'm afraid not."

"Thank you," Esquire said. "You've been very helpful."

She had no way of knowing that she'd be seeing the place where the man in the white fur hat kept his animal prisoners very soon—and right up close.

CHAPTER

Once she'd finished her potato-peel cider, Esquire took her time buttoning her tweed jacket and knotting her cream-colored scarf. Mr. Pepper had finished his second cider and was engaged in a spirited debate with the black cat over bird-feline politics—never a good topic to get into with a chicken if anyone hoped to get out of there by midnight. If Esquire tried to make him leave before he'd said his piece, though, she'd never hear the end of it.

All the same, the talk of the man in the white fur hat appeared to have spooked Mr. Pepper. When Esquire interrupted him, instead of scolding her like he usually would, he went quiet midsentence and hopped onto her shoulder. "Ready to go?" he asked, before tucking himself into her jacket.

Esquire paused, surprised, then gave Mr. Pepper's wobbly red coxcomb a pat. Maybe it was the cold making him keep snugglier than usual. Or maybe he shared the alarm she felt about this man in the white fur hat.

The black cat had offered that they could bunk with her and her kittens where they slept in the choir room of the town church, and Esquire would have taken her up on it. But time was of the essence for the young, trapped polar bear, and if that creature was alone and starving on an ice floe, Esquire wasn't going to sleep a wink. No, the only plan she could think of was to go back to that disagreeable human bar and see if this man with the white fur hat was still there—maybe Esquire could eavesdrop on his conversation, or even find out where he lived and tail him home.

It wasn't the greatest plan she'd ever come up with, but at least it was something.

Esquire was imagining how everything might go while she shimmied up the hole in the roof of the rat pub and into the mechanic's shop.

. . . And directly into a net.

She wasn't sure what was happening at first—she

sensed rope fibers, something she hadn't felt against her whiskers since back in her early days when she used to go fish burgling. Though Utqiagvik was a sea town, she was in a mechanic's shop. Why would there be a net *here*? For a moment she was totally baffled, pawing the ropes as she tried to find an opening. "What's going on out there?" came Mr. Pepper's muffled voice.

"Someone seems to have left a net on top of the exit, strangely enough!" Then she heard her own ridiculous words. "Oh no, Mr. Pepper. We're in a trap."

With a *rppt* sound, they were suddenly up in the air. The ropes stank of rotten fish, the smell so strong that Esquire nearly gagged. The pendulum feeling of rocking back and forth over the mechanic's floor didn't help matters at all.

She'd been in traps before and gotten herself out each time. First step was to climb to the top of the ropes. They were usually held up by a winch of some sort, and if she could just manage to get up there she could use her agile claws to cut herself free.

But when Esquire looked up, she gasped. The net wasn't being held by a device. It was being held by a human being.

A man in a white fur hat.

The mechanic's shop must have closed for the day; the only light on the man's face was from the Emergency Exit sign, which cast his features in cruel red. He peered at Esquire, surprise on his face . . . and something like delight, too.

He looked like someone who'd lucked into a purse of gold. "You *are* a fox wearing a suit," the man said, stroking the hairs that grew out of his nose. "And here I was, thinking I'd had too much to drink."

This is a tweed jacket, not a suit, Esquire thought in outrage. A suit was a jacket *and* pants. What kind of an imbecile was this human? And what kind of fox would wear pants? *That* was the crazy thought.

"What a curiosity," the man in the white fur hat said. "Where did you steal that suit from? And why would an animal decide to wear such a thing?" He glanced around, as if he were suddenly nervous that someone might steal his prize. But they were alone. Unfortunately.

While the man in the white fur hat licked his lips, Esquire gripped the net as best she could with her back claws so that she could wrap her front paws across her chest. It was the best way she could think of to keep the man from noticing that she had a rooster tucked under her jacket. So far so good—as long as Mr. Pepper kept his cool and didn't start fussing.

Even as she struggled to find some advantage, Esquire's heart sank. She couldn't figure a way out—this stranger was far bigger and stronger than she was, and the net's fibers were too thick to gnaw through quickly.

On top of everything else, she felt like an idiot. It was one thing to let herself get netted. But Mr. Pepper had been getting on her for years about wearing clothing in public. She'd grown up in a filthy den, though, and had worked hard to get as far as she had in life. She looked *good* in her tweed jacket!

All the same: if they made it out of this alive, Esquire Fox was going to be in *big* trouble with Mr. Pepper.

She debated whether to open her mouth and speak. She could try to argue with the man, to find out what he wanted. But showing a human that she could talk would break one of the primary rules of the Animal Rescue Agency, and of all animal-dom. Besides, if the man in the white fur hat had gotten an evil look in his eye when he saw a clothed fox on his hands, what lengths would he go to once he realized he had a *talking* clothed fox?

She heard a chittering sound, and saw a pair of mice on top of a toolbox, enjoying a big chunk of cheddar cheese—the very same pair of mice that had slinked away after word got out that the Animal Rescue Agency was on the job. When they saw Esquire staring at them, they squeaked in surprise and ran off, carrying the cheese between them.

Just as she'd suspected. She had been bought at a price.

It was too much. Esquire couldn't resist giving this man—and those traitorous mice—a piece of her mind, and found her big mouth opening despite her best intentions. Right as she was about to speak, though, a vision came to her of how upset Mr. Pepper would be if she went and broke her own rule. It was in that moment of hesitation that the man in the white fur hat hefted the net—Esquire and Mr. Pepper along with it—over his back. Her tailbones crunched painfully. It was all she could do to keep her forelegs extended so the net's ropes didn't squish Mr. Pepper.

Funny, though—her jacket was flat against her chest.

Mr. Pepper wasn't there.

"Mr. Pepper?" Esquire whispered urgently. "Where are you?"

She looked back behind them, and that's when she saw it. A rooster was in the middle of the snowy road, staring after her and the man in the white fur hat. Mr. Pepper hopped up and down, clearly doing all he could not to furiously squawk his head off and give his location away.

"How did you manage to slip out?" Esquire whispered to herself. She nimbly maneuvered in the net so she was upside down, and examined the bottom. Four of the net's rope fibers had been cleanly snipped, the work of some sharp implement. Like a chicken beak. Mr. Pepper, how I adore you! Esquire rejoiced to herself as she slipped her head through the opening, then let gravity drop the rest of her body soundlessly to the snow. Not risking a moment to find out whether the man in the white fur hat had noticed her escape, she stole through the night to join Mr. Pepper.

CHAPTER

E squire and Mr. Pepper huddled in the narrow space between a trash can and a brick wall.

"What kind of a fool fox barges right out of a tunnel without checking to see if there is a net tied up right across it? Answer me that!"

"Now, Mr. Pepper, what good will assigning blame do?" Esquire said. Did she have something else she'd meant to say to Mr. Pepper? A thank you, perhaps? She couldn't remember. "On with the mission. We have to rescue that polar bear cub."

Mr. Pepper broke off his outraged clucking. "Of course," he said soberly. "He probably doesn't know how to hunt for himself yet."

Esquire tucked Mr. Pepper into her jacket and darted through the shadows, periodically looking up at the cloud-shrouded moon to get her bearings. "Precisely," she said as she went. "We do have more information, at least. We have a culprit, and we know that the polar bear cub is floating in the sea north of here. A rescue is our first priority. But if that's still a few hours off, we'll need to get some supplies to him in the meantime."

"Yes," Mr. Pepper said. "That little cub must be famished."

Once she'd gotten them through a deserted lot at the edge of town, Esquire tossed back her head and made a strange and strangled call. "What in the world was that?" Mr. Pepper asked. "Are you sick?"

Esquire flicked her ears. "No! Are you telling me that didn't sound like a husky howl?"

Mr. Pepper shook his head so savagely that his coxcomb danced and wobbled. "It most certainly did not. And why in darnation would you want to howl like a husky?"

"You'll see in a minute, Mr. Pepper!" Esquire said. "Ta-da!"

Esquire stretched her forelegs out triumphantly, gesturing down the street. Mr. Pepper popped his head out of the jacket and stared. And stared. The moment went long. The moment went awkward. "What is it I'm supposed to see?" Mr. Pepper whispered.

"Just give it a minute, Mr. Pepper!" Esquire repeated, louder this time. "TA-DA!"

Snow drifted in front of a streetlight.

Then . . . finally!

Esquire heard the panting first, and then their husky operative hurtled around a corner, pink tongue lolling out of her mouth. The milk-crate sled bounced behind her, plowing through the snow. Esquire shook the crate free of debris, and then righted it. She was glad to see that her suitcase with the brass fasteners was still secured inside. "In we go!" she said brightly.

"I was afraid that was what was coming next," Mr. Pepper grumbled. "Traveling in a husky-powered crate is worse than on a dolphin-powered inner tube."

"You mean during our Barbados lionfish caper? That escape on a dolphin-powered inner tube was pure genius, Mr. Pepper!"

"Fox standards for 'pure genius' are highly suspect," Mr. Pepper said.

"To the peak!" Esquire said, scratching between the husky's ears with one paw as she used the other to point to the cliff overhanging the town, the same one they'd tumbled down to reach Utqiagvik in the first place.

The husky arf-ed and lurched into action, sending Esquire tumbling back into the crate. She reached out just in time to catch Mr. Pepper before he flew into a snowdrift. He squawked in indignation.

"Less squawking and more holding on, Mr. Pepper!" Esquire said joyfully. She'd been hoping they'd have a reason to take a second sled dog ride.

Mr. Pepper hopped to the floor of the milk crate, where he'd be shielded from the biting air. "I assume your furbrained plan is to head back up to the cliff and see if we can spot the polar bear cub?"

"Yes," Esquire shouted. "And there's nothing 'furbrained' about it! If you're not careful, Mr. Pepper, my self-esteem will take a hit one of these days."

"I'll eat my tail feathers the moment that happens!"

"Once we figure out precisely where the cub is, we'll decide how best to get to him," Esquire pressed on, wiping icicles from her ear fur. "Now, be a good chicken and get the binoculars out of my valise, would you?"

Mr. Pepper harrumphed and set to work. Even as the sled slalomed from side to side, the agile rooster managed to peck open the brass fasteners and emerge with binoculars. Actually, it was a set of children's opera glasses from the 1800s, but they were the only magnifiers Esquire had found that would fit over her narrow muzzle, and besides, she liked the handsome filigree detailing. "Have you ever noticed the little tree nymphs running along the outside?" Esquire asked. She held the glasses up to the moonlight, nearly tumbling out of the careening crate as she did.

"This is not the time, Esquire!" Mr. Pepper said through clenched beak.

"Right, right," Esquire replied, holding on to the edge of the sled with one forepaw and using the other to bring the glasses to her eyes.

The world bobbed and bounced too much for her to see anything useful. "I think I should wait until we stop moving," she yelled to Mr. Pepper.

"Of course you should," he said as he tucked himself back into the safety of Esquire's jacket.

"Of course I should," Esquire repeated to herself, chagrined. "Of course I should."

Huffing and panting, the husky finally drew to a stop on the moonlit mountain peak. Legs shaking with cold and fatigue, Esquire stepped out and untied the crate. Making sure Mr. Pepper was secure, she crept to the edge of the windswept cliff and raised the glasses to her eyes.

Seen through the binoculars' twin circles, the waves were tall and a forbiddingly dark gray blue, dotted in chunks of ice and white caps. "I don't see . . . oh, there he is. Poor little guy," Esquire said, focusing the image.

She had found a very wretched sight. A skinny polar bear cub was on a floe, fluffy ears pushed back against his head, claws deep into the ice to stop from being pitched over. Even though Esquire knew she couldn't actually hear anything this far away, she thought she could almost detect the mewling sound of the cub's cries.

She shook her head, letting the binoculars hang by their neck strap. "Can I look?" asked Mr. Pepper.

Esquire held the binoculars up to Mr. Pepper's face. "Ah yes, very tragic," Mr. Pepper said. He was looking in the wrong direction. Because of the way chicken heads are shaped, Mr. Pepper had never been able to use the binoculars, but Esquire knew better than to call him out on it.

"Unless we're willing to steal a human boat, it's hard to imagine rigging a seacraft that could manage those rough conditions," Esquire said.

"We are absolutely not stealing a boat," Mr. Pepper said. "Someone would come looking for it, and all we need is for them to spot a fox and a chicken going for a sail. That would be the end of the whole agency."

Esquire stamped her paws, trying to get feeling back into them. If they waited until the cub came to land, the man in the white fur hat would be waiting there, too, and the rescue would fail. But if they couldn't reach the poor little animal by sea . . . hmm. This was a pickle.

Until it was no longer a pickle. A smile crept over Esquire's face.

Mr. Pepper peered up from his hiding spot. "No. Absolutely not."

"You don't even know what I was thinking!" Esquire protested.

"You are not flying to that cub," Mr. Pepper said flatly.

Esquire threw her forelegs in the air. "And why not? This is a perfect launch point. There are good winds, and it will be a clear shot once it's daylight."

"You're forgetting that you don't own a plane."

"I could zoom right down," Esquire pressed on, ignoring Mr. Pepper. "I even packed my snazzy aviator goggles in the valise, just in case."

"No, you didn't. Well, you did, but then I removed them."

"And I put them back in," Esquire said proudly, raising her scarf up to her ears so it covered her grin.

"You wouldn't!"

"I most certainly would, because I most certainly did."

"Do you remember the last time you tried to fly? You wound up crashing us onto that desert island in the middle of the Indian Ocean. We were there for two weeks before that swordfish rescued us. Two weeks. I had to eat sand grubs to stay alive! Sand grubs!"

"I consider that a practice round," Esquire protested. "By now I must be a much better flier. I'm sure of it."

"I won't hear any more of this," Mr. Pepper said. "We will not be flying today."

Esquire tipped her head so she could stare Mr. Pepper right in the eye. "Perhaps you could just, um, fly down yourself. Being a bird and all."

Mr. Pepper's coxcomb wobbled in outrage. "That is not funny, Esquire Fox."

"All I'm saying is that we don't really have any other

options. Until chickens can fly, I suppose I'll just have to do the piloting myself."

"And where do you intend to find an aircraft?"

Esquire tapped a claw against her temple. "Leave that to me."

"What do you mean, 'Leave that to me'? You don't expect I'd let a fool like you plan this operation all by herself, do you?"

"I do, actually. Because you're needed elsewhere."

"Is that so?" Even while Mr. Pepper's coxcomb continued its irritated wobble, his chest feathers plumped out. He did enjoy being delegated important tasks.

"Yes," Esquire said, lifting Mr. Pepper from within her coat and nestling him deep in the warm fur on the husky's back. "That cub is scared and alone and has no idea that we're going to be rescuing him at dawn. Someone needs to go tell him that help is on its way and bring him some food to eat and water to drink."

"You know I can't fly, Esquire. That joke wasn't funny the first time around."

"It's true that you can't fly," Esquire said, "but you can make friends who can. There are bound to be snow geese around here. They're too small to fly the bear off the floe, but they can bring him some supplies. They have no love for polar bears, but I'm sure they'll do a favor for a sweet old rooster like you."

"Quite right," Mr. Pepper sniffed. "I expect they would."

"Okay, then!" Esquire said. "Time to go pilfer myself some airplane parts."

She patted the top of the husky's snout. "Do you know of any snow geese nearby?"

The dog arf-ed and pranced around in a circle. It struck Esquire all over again that this new field operative might not be the most sophisticated one the Animal Rescue Agency had ever had. But she was certainly one of the most dedicated. Esquire plucked Mr. Pepper from the dog's back and arranged him in the crate, tucking his tea-cozy coat in around his skinny legs. "Warm enough?" she asked.

"Quite," Mr. Pepper said bravely. "The winds aren't as bad as they were a few hours ago."

He crowed in surprise as the husky lurched into motion.

"Wait!" Esquire cried.

The dog stopped abruptly, nearly tipping the crate—and Mr. Pepper—over in the process.

"Mr. Pepper, please make sure of one thing," she

called to her dear delicious friend, worrying her paws together.

"What's that?" he asked.

"Please make doubly sure that *you* don't wind up being the meal that you bring the polar bear."

CHAPTER

Esquire cracked her paw knuckles, the sound muffled by her soft woolen gloves. She really couldn't be done with Utqiagvik soon enough—it was no place for a red fox. It wouldn't even be a nice place for an arctic fox, for that matter. It was full of houses, and between those houses was dirty, sludgy snow or dirty, sludgy asphalt. Every street looked the same, because every street was ugly. Blech.

Alert to any sign of the man in the white fur hat, she hesitated in front of the mechanic's shop that led to the rat pub. Perhaps that friendly house cat would still be there, and she could help Esquire track down the parts to make herself an airplane. But the watering hole was where she'd been ratted out by those mice (hah!), so Esquire was leery of returning. Instead she stayed hidden outside, observing who came and went.

She cracked her knuckles some more. She'd like to give those treacherous mice a hunk of cheese—right to the face.

No one seemed to be coming and going from the rat pub, though, and time was ticking away. It was probably only a matter of hours until the cub would arrive at the shores of Utqiagvik and be captured.

Esquire remembered the cat saying that she lived in the choir room of the town church. Perhaps she could try there. It wouldn't be hard to find—a steeple towered over the town, at the end of the shoreline. Hunched over, Esquire reknotted her scarf, jammed her forepaws in her pockets, and slinked her way through the shadows.

She was stealthy, but not stealthy enough to escape at least one person's notice: eyes following her, staring out of a small window of the local bar.

Above those eyes was a white fur hat.

Esquire soon reached the town beach. She guessed that was the word for it, but no one would be sunbathing there anytime soon. It was more of a hardened rocky edge to the town, the cold sea lapping against it.

Fishing boats had frozen into the harbor in front of a kayak outfitter that looked long shuttered. Esquire considered snagging one of the kayaks and then thought better of it; there were probably only a few days a year when kayaking from here would be a good idea, and this was definitely not one of them. As she headed toward the church, Esquire snatched a loop of stinky rope from one of the fishing boats. Could prove useful. She'd return it once this adventure was over.

As she continued to the church, Esquire sensed movement behind her and whirled around. She couldn't see anyone, though. Snow was falling from the night sky; maybe that was the motion she'd detected. She continued on her way.

Even with her excellent night vision, it was hard to see much. Esquire drew her coat tighter, and wished she had Mr. Pepper with her. Even his bellyaching would be better than this awful quiet. *Maybe what you mean to say is that you miss me,* Esquire could imagine Mr. Pepper saying. She smiled. *Okay, Mr. Pepper, I miss you.*

As she sped toward the church, Esquire passed the town's drugstore. She paused, then on instinct decided to take a look. After scanning about to make sure no humans were around, she rattled the front door. Locked of course.

There was a window in back that, once she'd warmed the ice covering it with her haunches, opened just enough to let her in. A fox really could go anywhere she pleased.

Esquire prowled the dark aisles. No need to risk turning on the lights; her night vision gave her plenty of information. Moisturizers—no thanks. Painkillers—no. Magazines—maybe one of the home decorating ones, don't mind if I do. Cookies— sure, why not a couple? Paws full, cookie crumbs dotting her whiskers, but no closer to getting herself an air- craft, Esquire passed the last aisle.

Toys. Hmm. Potential.

She skirted past the soldiers and guns, past the board games and remote-controlled cars. Last were the kites. They had orange clearance stickers on them, and Esquire could understand why. It was hard to imagine much kite-flying weather in Utqiagvik. She selected the largest one she could find. It had a flam- ing skull on it, which wasn't quite her style, but the background was an army green that would bring out her eyes nicely.

An aircraft!

Esquire was so pleased with herself that she pinned the magazine and kite in her legpit and scampered to the window exit on all fours, like an ordinary fox might. Then she remembered herself and stood up on her hind legs before heading back out into human civilization. As she eased open the back window, she thought she saw a shape move on the other side of the glass. She froze. The shape vanished, and she heard an engine fade away. It had probably been just a truck passing by.

Esquire poked her head out the window, sneezing from the sudden cold invading her nostrils. The coast was clear. She scarfed the last of the cookies, tossed the kite and home decorating magazine to the ground, and hopped silently to the snowy street.

She had her aircraft now. Once she reached the polar bear cub, she'd need a way to direct the floe. She remembered the kayaks lined up by the town beach. Where there were kayaks, there were sure to be paddles.

Even Mr. Pepper couldn't complain once he'd heard about this masterful plan. She'd figured it out all by herself and didn't need to involve the house cat! Mr. Pepper had little trust for felines and wouldn't have approved. Whistling, Esquire took the fastest route down to the waterfront.

All the while, the man in the white fur hat watched.

CHAPTER

By now, Esquire felt she knew Utqiaġvik's streets pretty well. Even in the dark of night, she moved confidently, picking the smaller streets where she could be sure there were fewer streetlights. Just a few more blocks, and then she'd be on her way up to the summit where Mr. Pepper and the husky would be waiting.

Yes! Nearly there. She'd reached the abandoned lot that was the last remnant of human civilization before she'd be back to wonderful wilderness. Esquire scurried up the chain-link fence and dropped to the icy ground on the far side, then stole across the snow.

A figure caught her eye, right in the middle of the lot. Now, that was strange . . . why was Mr. Pepper *here*?

He was seated quietly, right beneath the pool of light from a streetlamp. It was odd enough that he was relaxing in a freezing abandoned lot, when they were supposed to meet on the clifftop. Even odder was that he was facing away from Utqiagvik.

But it was unmistakably Mr. Pepper. He was even wearing his tea-cozy coat.

Maybe he'd come down because he missed Esquire and had fallen asleep while he was waiting. Esquire grinned, ready to give him a good ribbing.

"Hi there, Mr. Pepper," Esquire whispered urgently as she neared.

The rooster didn't turn around. He just sort of shook a little.

Finally, Esquire was beside him. She nudged his tea cozy with her paw. "Did you fall as—oh!"

She'd gotten around to the front. There, in Mr. Pepper's beak, was a wadded-up sock.

"Mr. Pepper, why did you try to eat someone's *sock*?"

The rooster's eyes were wide in panic. Esquire could see now why he hadn't gotten up. His legs were bound together with rope. Something clicked for Esquire. "Oh dear."

She looked up. "Yep, there it is."

A net—thicker and sturdier this time—flew through the air and landed on Esquire and Mr. Pepper both.

A second time. She'd let herself get trapped a second time!

"So," Esquire whispered to the black-footed kittiwake in the cage beside hers, "what are you in for?"

Every kittiwake Esquire had ever met had been talkative and goofy, with personalities to match their clown-like feet, but this bird didn't answer. He stared at the bare floor of his cage, rocking back and forth. He wasn't the only one, either. All the animals in this warehouse were showing signs of sadness, pacing in circles or staring listlessly or not responding even when a charming lady fox in a custom tweed jacket asked them a question.

"This is a very bad place," Esquire whispered to Mr. Pepper. "I don't like it one bit."

"I can sense the bad vibes even inside your jacket," Mr. Pepper whispered back. "It's getting stuffy in here, by the way."

"We're in an unheated warehouse," Esquire said, teeth chattering. "Even if it weren't freezing, I think you should stay hidden in case the man in the white fur hat comes back. He seemed equally excited to have a rooster in a strawberry apron and a tea-cozy coat as he was to have a fox in a tweed jacket. I hate to think what he has in mind for us."

"At least he only had one cage left and had to dump us in together," Mr. Pepper said. He clucked. "I'm sorry I let myself get caught, Esquire. We had to pass by town on our way to the snow geese, and it seems the man in the white fur hat was lying in wait. When he jumped out and surprised us, I ran in the wrong direction. One of my earmuffs had fallen over my eye. Good thing the husky managed to get away."

"Don't give it another thought, Mr. Pepper," Esquire said, distracted. She turned to the ermine in the cage on the other side of her. "What are you in for?"

"None of them will talk to you," rumbled a deep voice from the far end of the warehouse. "They've been in here too long. They've given up hope."

Esquire pressed herself against the bars of her cage. Across the bleak open space of the drafty warehouse, she could just make out a large moving shape, pressing against the bars of its own steel enclosure. It made a clacking noise, because the creature had two big tusks.

"Giving up never got anyone anywhere," Esquire called out to the walrus.

"Once you discover that nothing you can do will get you free, you'll give up, too," the walrus bellowed.

"Shh," Mr. Pepper squawked from within Esquire's jacket. "The man in the white fur hat will hear you!"

"What worse could he do to me?" the walrus groaned. "He's already hauled me away from my family. He's already taken my freedom."

Esquire sat on the cold concrete floor, sticking her

limbs out between her cage's bars. "Why has he done this to us? What's he getting out of it?"

"What does it matter?" the walrus said. "Knowing the reason why wouldn't do anything to change our situation. Haven't you noticed? It's becoming harder and harder to avoid humans. Soon there will be no land left for animals at all."

"Your gloom is positively exhausting," Esquire sniffed.

"You'll be as gloomy as I am soon enough."

"Charming thought," Esquire whispered to herself as she chewed on her claws. It was a bad habit that Mr. Pepper was always reprimanding her for, but he was tucked away in her jacket and couldn't see it. So there.

Esquire had brooded for only a few minutes before the door opened and the man in the white fur hat came through. "Hello, my pets!" he called out. The scant light in the warehouse exaggerated the caverns of his sallow cheeks.

The animals stayed quiet. All, that is, except the walrus, who gave a mournful bellow.

The man in the white fur hat ripped a prod from the wall and jabbed it between the bars of the walrus's cage. A blue spark, then the beast's bellow turned from one of sadness to one of pain. All the while the walrus kept its watering eyes trained on Esquire, as if to say *Now do you see what happens when we speak up?*

"What a beastly human," Esquire whispered, instinctively pulling back her lips to display her sharp teeth.

"Don't you dare say anything more," Mr. Pepper scolded from within Esquire's coat. "Last thing we need is for him to realize you can talk."

Esquire held quiet as the man returned to the doorway and struggled through, dragging something large and bulky. Once it finally reached a well of dim light, Esquire could see it was a new cage, this one with even thicker bars than the walrus's. Thick enough to restrain the mightiest animal.

Thick enough to restrain a polar bear.

At least it's empty, Esquire thought.

Once he'd slotted the cage in beside the others, the man in the white fur hat took a moment to catch his breath, staring down each of his listless prisoners in turn. He'd just fixed his cruel gaze on Esquire when his phone rang. As he drew it from his pocket, Esquire pressed her face against the bars of her cage so her sensitive ears could pick up what he said. Of course, like most humans, the man didn't realize that animals could understand his words, so he made no effort to hide them. "Once the bear's ice floe arrives, I'll load the truck and head down to the zoo in Florida . . . of course! Most of these suckers will die on the way down there, but as long as the polar bear makes it, the money will be worth it . . . yep . . . I know, it's too hot down there, their last one died as soon as summer hit, and this one will wind up the same way, but that's their problem."

Esquire looked at the empty cage. Soon there would be a young animal inside, desperately missing his mother. If the cub even survived long enough to be caged. Esquire rattled the bars of her own prison in fury, then shrank back when the man in the white fur hat glanced her way. Whoops. Play it cool, Esquire.

He continued his phone conversation. "I know, that would be a lot easier . . . stupid laws, that's why. The authorities would stop me if I seized a polar bear from the wild and brought it into the states. But if an orphan shows up in Utqiagvik, with its mother nowhere to be found, then I can come forward and offer to rescue it. Everyone will be so relieved that I've found a nice zoo home for it . . . I know, I'm pretty proud of the plan myself . . . the cub's floe should be arriving in about two hours."

The depressed kittiwake next to Esquire finally

moved, clacking his beak in anger. "Shh," Esquire whispered. "Do you mind? I'm trying to get some spying done!"

The kittiwake's beak kept clacking. Esquire startled when she realized that he was saying words. "Keys," he said in a wheezy sort of shriek. "Caaaage keeeys."

"What are you on about?" Esquire asked. "Oh!" That's when she saw that, sure enough, a ring of keys was attached to the man in the white fur hat's belt loop.

But what good were keys if Esquire couldn't get to them? The man in the white fur hat clearly wasn't stupid; the bars of her cage were spaced narrowly enough that she couldn't slip through.

"Keys?" asked Mr. Pepper, his head popping up from within Esquire's tweed jacket. "Did someone say 'keys'? Allow me!"

Without waiting for a response, the small rooster promptly hopped to the freezing concrete and waddled out between the bars of Esquire's cage. His teapot cozy got stuck, falling onto the cage floor behind him.

The bars were narrow enough to keep Esquire inside. But the man in the white fur hat hadn't had a spare cage small enough to keep in a bantam rooster like Mr. Pepper.

It was far too cold for Mr. Pepper to be out, especially

without his quilted teapot cozy. "Stop," Esquire hissed, as she plucked up the chicken coat and tucked it into her jacket and away from view.

There's no dissuading a rooster on a mission, though. Mr. Pepper strutted into the shadows along the warehouse wall just as the man in the white fur hat looked over at his hissing fox prisoner. "You won't be heading to the zoo, my pretty. I'm not sure what to do with my fox in the suit yet."

It's not a suit. It's a jacket! To keep the man's attention distracted from Mr. Pepper, Esquire went full animal. She hissed and snarled, hurling herself dramatically against her cage bars. It was a disgusting and uncivilized display. But effectively distracting! And maybe even a little therapeutic.

The man's eyes widened as he spoke into his phone one last time. "I'll call you back later. I think I might have a rabid animal on my hands."

Rabid? Excuse me! But Esquire kept up her performance, doing backflips and scratching her claws against the bars of her cage.

The man in the white fur hat yanked the prod down from the wall and stepped toward Esquire. He sparked it threateningly. "Settle down, you vixen."

Vixen. Ugh. It was Esquire's least favorite word. She

kept up her snarling, though, since through the man's ankles she could see the tail feathers of a certain rooster she knew.

Mr. Pepper's coxcomb was already rimmed in frost, and his frozen claws clattered uncoordinatedly over the concrete floor as he made his way toward the man.

Esquire had to keep drawing the man's attention. In a fit of inspiration she started to howl, throwing her head back. She never allowed herself to do anything so grotesque as howl under normal circumstances, but this was a special case.

Strawberry apron ruffles fluttering around him, Mr. Pepper reached the man. He limbered up his wings, preparing to leap.

Chickens were not the world's best fliers, but they could still use their wings in bursts to get some good hang time. Mr. Pepper hopped and—miracle!—managed to clamp the man's key ring in his beak on the first try.

Unfortunately, the keys were still attached to his belt loop.

Eyes wide in alarm, Mr. Pepper kept his beak clamped on the key ring, hanging from the man's waist like a pocket watch. He was light enough that the man wouldn't notice. At least Esquire hoped so.

As Mr. Pepper swung from the man's belt, the tension clearly became just too great for the fiery old bird. He couldn't stop himself from letting out a squawk.

Alerted by the noise, the man whirled around. Of course Mr. Pepper was still attached to the belt loop and so whirled right with him, remaining out of view on the man's backside. It wouldn't be long before the man discovered the rooster clamped on to him, though.

Esquire had to do something drastic. So she stopped snarling and started speaking. "Yoo-hoo, Mister Animal Trafficker, I'm a talking fox!" Hmm, Esquire thought. I'll have to work on my catchphrases.

The man in the white fur hat froze and slowly turned toward Esquire, all his attention on her even as Mr. Pepper let out more squawks from his backside. "Did you just . . . speak?" he asked.

"Of course I did," Esquire said, crossing her forelegs smartly and tapping the side of her head. "Who else would it be? I don't know why humans go on and on about how intelligent they are."

It did the trick. The man was flabbergasted, hands over his mouth.

Mr. Pepper let go of the ring and beat his wings, managing to hover in the air for a brief instant, just long enough to get his beak around the belt loop attaching the keys and snip clean through it.

Esquire watched the keys tumble through the air as if in slow motion. The moment the man heard the sound of them striking the concrete he'd know what Mr. Pepper was up to . . .

. . . but the rooster dropped from the air just in time, landing beneath the keys so they fell into the soft plumage of his chest.

"It's a pleasure to meet you," Esquire said to the man in the white fur hat, keeping up a carnival smile despite the horror tightening her chest at his greedy expression. "I'm looking forward to working together."

"Forget the polar bear cub! This changes everything," the man said, stroking his hairy chin as he grinned at his lucky turn. He narrowed his eyes. "You're a golden swan. I'm going to need to go borrow an extra padlock for your cage."

"It's not 'the golden swan,' you imbecile," Esquire said haughtily. "It's 'the goose that lays the golden eggs.'"

The man in the white fur hat took another step toward Esquire, rubbing his hands together hungrily. Then he seemed to remember what he'd just said about borrowing an extra padlock, and sprinted through the warehouse, back toward the door—in the process nearly squashing Mr. Pepper flat to the floor. As it was, the man's boot landed just beside Mr. Pepper's delicate head. The rooster made another squawk, which the man in the white fur hat might have heard if he hadn't been in such a hurry.

The warehouse door slammed.

Mr. Pepper risked raising his head to look Esquire's way. Trembling with the cold, he nevertheless lifted the ring of keys in one clawed foot, victorious.

"If you don't mind, Mr. Pepper," Esquire said, "let's get opening these cages sooner rather than later."

CHAPTER

Esquire and Mr. Pepper stood on either side of the warehouse's exit, ushering through a stream of depressed animals.

Esquire had never really been the connect-with-your-feelings type, but seeing the drawn faces in the procession got her to dig deep. "Go eat some fish, kittiwake, you'll feel better in a few days . . . go now, ermine, I'm sure your family will take care of you until you're back to your old self . . . I know what you're feeling, walrus, but animals do recover after being caged, it just takes time, be good to yourself in the meantime."

It was as if Esquire weren't even there, as if she weren't giving good advice on matters of the heart. The animals didn't respond, just hurried into the frigid night, never looking back.

The doorway was a tight squeeze for the walrus, but even as he got stuck he didn't slow down, just popped on through like a cork leaving a champagne bottle. "Excuse me!" Esquire said as she leaped out of the way. She and Mr. Pepper watched the hefty creature disappear into the night without even a goodbye.

"Animals seem quite rude this far north," Mr. Pepper huffed. He probably crossed his wings, but Esquire couldn't tell because he had his tea cozy back on. "I didn't expect you to bill them for their rescue, but I did expect at least a moment of gratitude."

"They're scared the man in the white fur hat will be back and that they'll be caught all over again. Can't blame them for rushing off after what they've been through." Esquire tucked Mr. Pepper into her jacket before pulling her scarf around her ears and creeping into the corner of the warehouse, where the man in the white fur hat had stashed her aviation supplies. "No time for outrage, Mr. Pepper. I'd rather not fall back into that horrible man's clutches, either."

Mr. Pepper's voice continued unabated, though the sound was now muffled by Esquire's tweed. "And why did you go suggesting that kittiwake eat some fish? We don't want to ruin our reputation with the local sea creatures, not when those sea creatures might potentially be our next clients. Billing, Esquire, a business can't run without *billing its customers.*"

"Quite right, yes, understood," Esquire said into her lapel as she stole into the night.

CHAPTER

Esquire made her way up to the mountaintop with a spring in her step. Despite the cutting nighttime winds and the fact that she was lugging a rooster, a large kite, and a kayak paddle (not to mention a home decorating magazine) with her, she was filled with excitement. This was going to be amazing!

The husky was patiently waiting at the clifftop. *Very* patiently. So patient, in fact, that she had fallen asleep. At the sound of the dog's snoring, Mr. Pepper hopped out of Esquire's jacket and huddled himself into her soft fur, only his beak and eyes visible within the riot of silver coat, icicles forming wherever the rooster's breath landed.

Esquire dropped her supplies triumphantly in front of them. "How about *this*?"

Mr. Pepper clucked. "I was wondering what that pile of rubbish was in the corner of the warehouse. What kind of fool scheme are you onto?"

"What are you talking about?" Esquire asked, lips pulling back from her teeth despite her best efforts not to appear stung. "This is the very aircraft we need! I tracked it down at great personal risk."

"That is not an aircraft," Mr. Pepper retorted. "It is a *kite*."

"Let's split the difference and call it a glider," Esquire said, trying to relocate the good feeling she'd had only a moment ago. "Look, see!" She unfurled one wing and held it beside her face. "The color even brings out the green of my eyes!"

"The flaming skull on the back perfectly captures my feelings about where this will all lead," Mr. Pepper said.

Esquire shivered. "That's just silly. Haven't you noticed how strong the winds are up here? They'll carry me far enough."

"They'll carry you far, I believe that. But in which direction is another concern entirely." With that, Mr. Pepper gave a cock-a-doodle-do. The loud noise startled the husky out of her nap. She went into a barking fit, sending Mr. Pepper tumbling to the ground.

Esquire helped him to his feet. "Did you manage to plan the airlift of food before the man in the white fur hat caught you?" she asked.

Once he'd recovered his dignity, Mr. Pepper clucked proudly. "No. He caught me on the way to the snow geese."

"You didn't plan the airlift? Then why do you look so pleased with yourself?"

"I got the final piece in place while we were freeing the prisoners."

"I don't understand, Mr. Pepper."

"I won't even need to explain, because you're about to see what I mean!"

Esquire looked out over the water, where she saw a bird approaching through the dark sky. She started salivating—though she'd given up eating other animals years before, she'd had a real soft spot for seabirds back in the day—but stopped when the animal landed and she saw it was a gull with distinctive clown-like black feet.

"The kittiwake!" Esquire exclaimed.

"Yes, I aaaam!" the gull said, tapping his beak in the air excitedly, speaking the raucous dialect of all seabirds. "And I'd liiiiike to report that the suppliiiiies drop went perrrrrrfectly. The little cub thanked meeeee, and didn't eeeeeven seem to miiiiind that the only waaaaay for meeeee to carrrrrrry the fooooood was to swalloooooow it and then regurrrrrrrgitate it in front of him."

"I'm so glad!" Esquire said. "What was the food, by the way?"

"Oh, that. I had to give him almost all of your mushroom jerky ration," Mr. Pepper said.

Esquire shrugged. "I'm sure he needs it more than I do."

The kittiwake cawed. "Heeeeee's in baaaaad shape. You have to get there as soooooooon as you cannnn."

Esquire nodded, snapping the aviator goggles over her eyes. "Dawn is nearly here, so there's no more time to lose."

"Before you goooooo, I just want to saaaaay thank you," the kittiwake squawked. "I didn't have it in meeeee to find the worrrrrds back in that horrrrrrrible prison, but I'm verrrrrry graaaaaaateful. We all arrrrre."

"Lovely, lovely, you're welcome," Esquire said distractedly as she tightened her scarf and yanked her hat as tight as she could over her ears. "How do I look?"

"How do you *look*?" Mr. Pepper squawked. "Just worry about keeping warm, not how you look!"

Esquire rolled her eyes, and double-checked her

goggles. "There's the pale light of dawn, dear ones! Now is the moment for utmost bravery—we've got a polar bear cub to rescue!"

As she stood at the edge of the mountaintop, peering at the icy waves far below, Esquire inflated with the thrill of adventure. Despite Mr. Pepper's protests to the contrary, she had a snazzy glider, goggles, and a perfect plan. What could go wrong?

Esquire neatly looped her forelegs through the wings of the kite. As she held them out, she breathed in the scent of ocean air rising up the cliff . . . and promptly went sailing backward.

The first thing Esquire saw when she picked herself out of the snowdrift was Mr. Pepper, shaking his head and clucking. "It's unfortunate the paddles are too heavy for the kittiwake to fly them down instead. You know, since he can actually *fly*."

Esquire held up her paw to stop him before he could say any more. "I don't want to hear from doubters, Mr. Pepper!"

Mr. Pepper approached the husky. "Would you mind giving Esquire a running start?" he asked.

The dog stopped barking and inclined her head. "You know," Mr. Pepper said, flapping his wings and then pointing to Esquire. "Help her fly?"

The husky barked, nodded, turned a few quick circles, then fell dizzily into the snow.

The thrill of adventure had dampened a bit, but Esquire nonetheless adjusted her aviator goggles and clambered onto the husky's back. She unfurled the kite's wings. "Okay, I'll count down. Three, two—"

The husky raced to the edge of the mountaintop. The wind filled the kite as she went, and Esquire was lifted from the dog's back.

"One!" Esquire called. It was a little late, though, since she had already launched into the air—and was plummeting to the icy sea below.

CHAPTER

Hmm. I appear to be falling, when I really ought to be flying, Esquire thought as her ears and nose filled with frigid air.

She shifted her body, trying to angle it so that the kite wings could better catch the wind. All that did, though, was make her hit a crosscurrent . . . which closed the kite right up. Esquire tried to muscle her forelegs away from her sides, but those winds were *strong*.

Now she was zooming down to the water. Positively zooming. This was not good.

Esquire peered at the iron sea below, at its ice and forbidding swells. It was good that she had her aviator goggles on, or she wouldn't have been able to see a thing. As it was, her view of the sea trembled as the wind shuddered the glass.

Initially she'd been grinning from the thrill of the flight, but as she continued to drop, the grin dropped. If she hit the sea at this speed, she'd die.

Esquire frantically beat her forelegs, trying to get some lift. She was basically in the shape of a spear, her already aerodynamic fox body made even sleeker by the rushing air. Strangely, even though these might have been the last few seconds of her life, Esquire found herself thinking of Mr. Pepper. Maybe this is what it feels like to be a chicken, beating your wings but not flying.

The sea rushed ever closer. Only a few seconds until impact now. Esquire could see individual chunks of ice, foam on the ferocious wave caps, a startled gull looking up at the plummeting fox with the folded-up wings.

As Esquire arrowed closer and closer to the surface, instinct took over. Like she'd once done when falling from a medieval tower in Bologna, Esquire rolled onto her back, extending her legs and all her hair, so she generated maximum wind resistance. Who knows—it had worked in Italy!

Her free fall became more turbulent. Unexpectedly, with a glorious *phht* sound, the kite unfurled and caught air. The sudden loss of acceleration made Esquire feel like she was flung upward, her gut pushing against the front of her rib cage.

She was flying! Esquire the Aviator!

The kite held her forelegs out, so she couldn't even see them as she looked down. Her view was all sky and sea. Wind filled the kite wings, and by moving one leg or the other, Esquire was able to steer. She rocked her kite—No, her *glider*! Her *aircraft*!—back and forth, then arched her back to catch the wind shearing up from a tall wave. She shot up into the air, almost to the height of the mountaintop. "Hello! Look at me!" she screamed in the direction of Mr. Pepper and the husky.

She was almost sure she heard the rapid barking of a husky and a rooster giving a triumphant cock-a-doodle-do. Mr. Pepper's voice sure could carry.

Esquire whooped and did a barrel roll in response, imagining how very impressive the flaming skull must look as it turned over and over in the glittering dawn light.

Okay, back to business. *Rescue* business. Esquire scanned the waves, looking at each of the ice floes to see if she could spot a bear cub. It wasn't easy, since polar bears are nearly the color of ice, and the dawn gave her only partial light—and her aviator goggles had developed a layer of frost.

Esquire cast her thoughts back to the clifftop. With the binoculars, she'd spotted the bear a few inches to the right of the rising sun, which meant she should aim more leftward now—and there he was!

The poor little creature was still holding on for dear life, all four sets of claws digging into the ice. His face was pressed against the floe, so Esquire couldn't see his expression. One thing was unmistakable, though—he was exhausted.

She couldn't fly straight to him, as she didn't have enough altitude—she'd crash into the sea. Instead Esquire aimed for another updraft, soaring nearly straight up before she redirected back to the floe. It might take a couple of minutes for the glider to coast there, but she'd be able to control the descent, circling if she needed to so she could land gently beside the cub.

Now that she'd caught on to how to use the glider, Esquire relaxed into her flight, enjoying the feeling of wind between her hairs, tickling even the spaces between her claws. Foxes should fly more often. Wait, a flying fox, wasn't that a thing?

Caught in her thoughts, Esquire almost didn't notice an odd vibration in her wings. She couldn't help but give the glider her full attention, though, when one of its ribs fell out, tumbling over and over before plinking into the sea far below. The kite began to flap alarmingly.

In front of Esquire's eyes, that first rib was followed by a second.

Esquire looked up, trying to figure out what was happening to her aircraft. She was just in time to watch another seam in the kite unthread and rip open in the wind, releasing a third rib. Then a fourth. Now there were none left. Unsupported, the wings' fabric flapped wildly.

Why would they all fall out? It seemed impossible!

Esquire began to pump her forelegs, hoping that might help her catch more air. But the wings gave one last mighty flap, then folded up entirely. The rescue paddles, strapped to the spine of the kite, flipped out into the sky and dropped into the sea. Gone, gone, gone.

She was no longer Esquire the Aviator. She was just an ordinary red fox who had spent a few seconds in the center of the sky. Soon she would be a drowned fox at the bottom of the sea.

Mr. Pepper would be so disappointed in her.

Panicked, Esquire started running through the air on all fours.

But running doesn't work in the air. All she did was scream and fall.

The water rose to meet her, impossibly fast. Oh my, this is going to be very cold, was Esquire's last thought before she smacked into the surface.

Hitting water this fast was like slamming into solid earth. Esquire struck headfirst, her ears filling with a horrible *thwack* as red painted her vision and her body roared in pain. Then all was black.

Her last thoughts? That she'd failed.

CHAPTER

The world had gone so dark and so cold. She had no idea how long she was under the surface; all of time smooshed into a single point.

Then there were teeth around her neck.

"No," Esquire said weakly. "Let me go."

The teeth pulled on her nape; they were scraping the top of her head.

Something was trying to eat her. And not doing a great job of it.

Was it the man in the white fur hat? That didn't sound right.

It was so very cold, too cold to fight. Esquire feebly batted her claws in the air. When her paws hit fur, they couldn't even move the hair, much less the animal underneath it.

She managed to open her eyes. White fur, white ice, gray sea. It *was* the man in the white fur hat! Though her body was screaming at her to fall asleep, she forced her eyes open further.

She was on the floe.

She was on the floe, and she was not alone.

She was on the floe, she was not alone, and she was not with the man in the white fur hat.

She was on the floe, she was not alone, and she was with a polar bear cub.

She was on the floe, she was not alone, and she was with a polar bear cub that was trying to *eat* her!

"Stop," she murmured, trying and failing to get to her paws. "Don't eat me. I'm here to *rescue* you."

The polar bear cub leaned back, head cocked, struggling to keep his balance as he did. "You're *what?*"

A fit of shivering overtook Esquire. "Just . . . don't . . . eat . . . me . . . at least . . . not before . . . I explain."

"I wasn't eating you!" the cub protested. "I was licking the seawater off you before it froze!"

Esquire stared back at him, shivering uncontrollably. There was something she thought to say back to the cub, but she was so cold and startled that the thought vanished before she could speak it.

"Mom and I have only ever eaten seals. Well, and maybe some birds," the cub said. "Not strange orange dogs wearing glasses and flying in on flaming skulls."

"Oh!" Esquire said, pride creeping into her voice even as her teeth chattered more and more. "You . . . noticed my . . . skull?"

"More than that! I managed to paddle this floe over to save you." The cub flopped to the ice, head between his paws. "I'm even more tired now than I was before."

"*You* saved *me*?" Esquire said.

"I'm not sure yet. You still might die."

"Oh," Esquire said, both ashamed and oddly heartened. She shook her head, to clear it. "I'd rather not do that."

The polar bear cub lifted a forelimb. "Then come snuggle. Polar bears are very warm."

Esquire looked at the cub's furry belly. It certainly did seem snuggly. But he was one of the world's greatest predators, even if a very cute one. "Are you *sure* you don't want to eat me?"

The cub scratched behind one of his furry ears. "*Should* I want to eat you?"

"No," Esquire said hastily as she tucked into the cub's side, instantly warmed when he pulled her in close. "Oh my. You're right. This is very nice."

"So why were you flying in front of the sun on a flaming skull?" the cub asked.

"I was coming to save you, until of course you had to save me. My name is Esquire Fox, of the Animal Rescue Agency. I'm pretty good at it, too. The rescuing part. At least usually."

"I'm Little Claws. A man in a white fur hat blew something up, and I got trapped on this hunk of ice."

"Yes, I know all about the man in the white fur hat," Esquire said. "He's waiting for us to arrive on the mainland, and once he does he'll 'rescue' you and then sell you to a zoo in Miami. But we won't let that happen."

"Good!" the cub said, sitting up. "I don't want to go to a zoo in Miami. I want to go home to my mom."

"Please put that warm leg back over me," Esquire said.

"Sorry." The cub replaced the leg, and Esquire basked in the delicious warmth. Her tweed jacket was probably wrinkling, but even that didn't matter under the circumstances. "Where's Miami?" the cub asked.

"Far away. Nowhere any polar bears should be going."

"So . . . how were you going to rescue me?" the cub asked.

"With the—oh dear. I don't suppose you saw any paddles plop into the ocean around here?"

The cub shifted to one side. "Do you mean like this?"

Esquire looked. There was half a paddle—it must have broken in two when it struck the water. At least this was the wide paddling part and not the narrow holding part. Slightly more useful. "There were supposed to be two paddles, and they were supposed to be intact. We were going to use them to row you back north, away from Utqiagvik, so you wouldn't fall into the trafficker's clutches."

Little Claws shut his eyes. "I miss my mom."

"Your mother loves you very much," Esquire said. "She tried to save you herself, but she needed help. We'll get you back to her, I'll make sure of it."

Esquire looked toward the sun rising over Utqiagvik. The broken paddle wasn't going to be much use, which meant now she was just as trapped as the polar bear cub. It didn't seem likely she'd be doing any rescuing—in fact, the man in the white fur hat was going to get double his profit, now that he'd be able to seize the polar bear cub *and* the talking fox in the tweed jacket.

Esquire mustered up as much dignity as she could. "Animal Rescue Agency, at your service."

CHAPTER

Esquire examined the cliff face through her binoculars. Mr. Pepper and the husky were still there, staring out hopefully. Mr. Pepper had his wing in front of his eyes, shielding the sun to better spy where Esquire had gone. He was looking the wrong way, though—he must have lost track of Esquire. Eventually the rooster shook his head sadly and got back in the crate sled. The husky bounded down the mountain, pulling Mr. Pepper out of view.

Esquire sighed and let the binoculars drop around her neck. "I don't suppose you have a flare around here?" she asked Little Claws.

"What's a *flare*? Can we eat it? I'm so hungry. All

I've had to eat was that little pile of goo the kittiwake regurgitated."

"You knew what a skull was, but not a flare?"

"We have skulls in the Arctic!"

Esquire sighed again. A cub should get to live his wild life with a full belly, never needing to know what a rescue flare was, what a human looked like up close, and certainly not what a cage looked like from the inside. Esquire had been searching for years for a motto for the Animal Rescue Agency. Perhaps "To each animal, the right to live its natural life" would be a good one.

Bringing the binoculars back up, Esquire looked toward Utqiagvik.

The man in the white fur hat was waiting.

He stood at the shore outside town, his own binoculars up to his eyes, staring right back. The man gave a sinister wave, as if to tell Esquire she might as well give up. He had a flatbed truck behind him, filled with nets and rifles and other cruel-looking devices that Esquire couldn't identify. Next to him was a machine with a whirling flag on top that shifted with the wind—the contraption was probably how he was measuring the currents, to make sure he was in the precise spot where the floe would land so he could begin his "rescue" to the zoo in Miami.

"Do you see him?" Little Claws asked.

Esquire considered hiding the truth from the cub. She'd heard that's what you were supposed to do with the young, but Esquire knew that she always wanted the truth, and would have especially wanted the whole truth back when she was a kit. "Yes, he's there. But we're going to do our best to stop him from getting you. And me, for that matter."

Little Claws staggered to all fours and bared his teeth. "I'll fight him!"

He fell almost as soon as he stood, digging his claws into the floe to stop from being cast into the sea. In the upheaval, his bones showed even more starkly through his sparse fur. Though Little Claws hadn't complained, Esquire knew he hadn't eaten for months. He wouldn't be fighting anyone anytime soon. Despite that, she patted him on the head. "I'm glad I have you here to protect me."

"You don't mean that," Little Claws said, closing his eyes in misery. "I just want to go home to my mother. It's so hot this far south."

Esquire wouldn't have put it that way—she was

still shivering, even after Little Claws warmed her. She drew her wet tweed jacket tighter around her, snuggled down as best she could into the cub's belly. She hated the sight of his drooping ears.

She drew back away from Little Claws and took up the broken paddle. Leaning as far over the sea as she dared, she began to stroke. It didn't seem to be having any effect at all.

"That's never going to work," Little Claws moaned.

She had to distract him before despair took hold. "Tell me a story about your mom," she said as she continued to paddle.

The cub wailed. "The last thing I did was hit her in the face!"

"Really?" Esquire asked. "You hit her in the face?"

"Yes, I said it was spring and then, then I hit her in the face with a snowball!"

Esquire smiled. "With a *snowball*. I see. That's not so bad. I'm sure she knew you were playing. I wouldn't give it another thought."

"I get so mad at her sometimes, because I want to have a brother or sister to play with. But I'm not mad at her now, and I can't even tell her that."

"I'm sure she's very worried about you." Esquire

lifted the paddle up from the water and peered at it. It was doing nothing to change the floe's course. Maybe it had a hole in it or something.

"Do you think she'll rescue us?" Little Claws asked. "I've been looking for her."

"I'm sure she's been trying. Polar bears might be good swimmers, but once you were caught in this current it was too far for her to make it. We'll send her word once you're safe, and then find some way to get you back to her."

"What's *your* mom like?" Little Claws asked.

Esquire sat up in surprise, the binoculars bouncing against her chest. She started paddling again, to cover her reaction. "My mother? Well, there's not much to say about her."

"What do you mean? Everyone has something to say about their mother."

Esquire considered what to say next. "Well, I grew up in *very* different circumstances from how I live now. It's like another lifetime."

The cub's face went from expectant to disappointed. "Okay. I guess you're not going to tell me any stories about it."

Esquire's thoughts went to her rambunctious

littermates, always nipping at one another, that dank cave full of the smell of pee and the crunching of bloody bones, her mother snapping and snarling, not even bothering to name her kits, sending them out on their own the moment they'd weaned, into the harsh outside world where they could be attacked by any male foxes roving about. It was a horrible start to a life. How would that story be at all helpful to a despairing polar bear cub? "There's just not much to say," Esquire finally said.

"Oh," the cub said. "I imagined that you came from a long line of adventuring foxes, and that your mom introduced you to the rescuing life when you were my age."

Esquire's face brightened. "You know who did get me into this line of work? Mr. Pepper!"

"Is Mr. Pepper your father?"

Despite the cold and wet, despite being so powerless to stop their floe from its slow passage toward the man in the white fur hat, Esquire laughed. "No, Mr. Pepper isn't my father. He's a rooster!"

Little Claws nodded wisely. "I get it. This is the story of your favorite meal. I like this kind of story."

Esquire decided to give her aching muscles a break.

She licked a paw and ran it over the fur between her ears, sending a spray of ice crystals tinkling to the floe. She blew on her forepaws and slotted them into the damp fabric of her jacket pockets. "It could have turned out that way. But this story has an unexpected twist. Where to begin? First thing you need to know is that I was once perhaps the greatest chicken thief the world has ever known."

"That sounds amazing," Little Claws said. "I'm not even positive what a chicken is, but it sounds delicious."

Esquire smacked her lips. "Ever eaten a gull? A chicken is like that, only fifty times tastier. I haven't eaten one for many years, though."

"Wow. Why would you ever stop eating chickens?"

"That's where Mr. Pepper comes in. I was in the middle of a raid when my grappling hook came loose and I fell from a great height, right into the breeding center of a giant chicken farm. There were hens everywhere, clucking and panicking and pecking. Feathers left and right."

"Yum," Little Claws said.

"Normally it would be," Esquire said. "But I hit my head *really* hard. I nearly died. Once I could move, I got to my paws and saw that the hens were all in a corner, and a rooster stood in front of them, wings outstretched, beak open, shrieking his head off. He was challenging me!"

"Ooh, did you eat him?" Little Claws asked.

"No!" Esquire said. "This was Mr. Pepper. He was ready to fight to the death to save all of those hens. Of course he was a chicken and I was a fox. There's only one way that fight would have gone. Not much beaks and chicken legs can do against teeth and claws. Even though roosters do have a mean roundhouse kick."

"So you *did* eat him!"

"No, I didn't eat him—keep up with me, Little Claws. Mr. Pepper is my colleague. You'll meet him if all goes well. My mind was already a little scattered from the fall, and the way this rooster acted was so unusual. Normally they cower, and if they fight it's in a desperate, hopeless sort of way. Not Mr. Pepper, though. He was convinced I didn't have the right to eat him."

"Some birds are so uppity," Little Claws complained, shaking his head sadly.

"Maybe it was because I fell on my head," Esquire said, "but I believed him."

"Wow," Little Claws said. "You're weird."

"Yes," Esquire said, stroking her chin. "I suppose I am a little weird. I wound up liberating the very chickens I'd come to eat. I broke them out of the farm, and then told the rest of the foxes that they couldn't have them! It didn't go over well."

"I bet it didn't," Little Claws said. "I wouldn't like it if someone told me not to eat seals, because then I wouldn't have anything to eat at all."

"Yes. Now the fox syndicate has a warrant out for me, all because I left to pursue justice for mistreated animals. That sort of thing can make life very tricky for a fox who'd rather stay home and drink tea and listen to her jazz records."

"Well, *I'm* glad that you decided to help animals in distress," Little Claws said.

"I bet you'd prefer if I were a little better at it," Esquire said.

"That was definitely an interesting story, though," Little Claws said sleepily. "Say, are you ever tempted to eat Mr. Pepper anymore?"

Esquire brought the binoculars up to her eyes to check on the man in the white fur hat. He was still staring right back. Esquire bared her teeth at him, not that he could see. "I'm not, strangely enough," she finally responded to Little Claws as she took the paddle back up and stirred the water with it. "Ever since we started the Animal Rescue Agency, I haven't looked back. Eating is a habit, and there are actually good alternatives to meat out there. Mr. Pepper makes me this delicious mushroom jerky that satisfies my cravings. I think you've had some, but only after it was regurgitated by a kittiwake, which can't be good for the flavor. If I had some on me, I'd let you try it—oh, blast!"

Her paws had gotten too cold—the paddle slipped entirely out of her grasp. Not a huge loss, considering that it had done precisely nothing to alter their course toward the man in the white fur hat.

Esquire checked Little Claws's reaction to the loss of the paddle and discovered the cub was asleep. She snuggled down against the snoring cub, stroked the wet fur on his paw. "Rest up, little one," she whispered. "You're going to need all the strength you can muster."

CHAPTER

Esquire's limbs were aching with the cold, and a nagging deadly voice kept begging her to close her eyes and go to sleep, like the cub beside her. She bit her lip to keep herself awake. Esquire didn't have a nice thick pelt like his—if she fell asleep in this wet cold, it might be the sleep that lasted forever. If she managed to survive the hypothermia, she'd wake up in the clutches of the man in the white fur hat.

She brought the binoculars to her eyes to take one last look at the trafficker. They bounced and shook in her trembling grasp. As the floe neared, he took up a large net in one hand and what appeared to be a harpoon gun in the other. The significance was clear: if he didn't manage to capture Esquire and Little Claws alive, he'd bring home their pelts instead.

All the while, the floe tipped and rocked as it drifted toward the barren stretch of beach. The town was well out of sight, which meant the capture would happen in private; even if Esquire had hoped other humans might be inspired to help them, there were none around here to do so.

Esquire kneeled on the slippery ice and tried to paddle with her paw. It soon turned numb. Even if her kite hadn't mysteriously disintegrated, even if she'd managed to fly the paddles intact to the cub's floe, they still might not have been able to get to safety. The currents were too strong. Esquire stopped paddling and buried her nose in her chest, trying to blot out the world. Her plan had been terrible. Her agency had promised a rescue, and it wasn't going to deliver.

Even though he wasn't here, Mr. Pepper's voice rang out in Esquire's mind: *You fool fox! Sure, this was an idiotic plan—but it's* definitely *not going to succeed if you go belly-up in the middle of it!*

Esquire smiled despite herself. Even when he wasn't around, that rooster managed to be irritating. (Also, maybe she was going a little insane?)

When she looked up, she saw that the man in the

white fur hat was much closer than before. It wouldn't be more than fifteen minutes until they were in his clutches. "Come to father!" he yelled to Esquire and Little Claws, hefting the net in the air.

"Ew," Esquire mumbled under her breath. She elbowed Little Claws in the ribs. "Get up, small one, the moment is nearly here."

"Shh," Little Claws moaned in his sleep, rolling over. "It's not spring yet."

Esquire elbowed Little Claws harder. "Get up!"

Little Claws blinked his eyes open and peered around. "Mom?" Then he saw Esquire and the frigid sea. Esquire's heart dropped as she watched the hope fade from Little Claws's eyes.

"We're almost to shore, and the trafficker's getting his net ready," Esquire hissed. "We can't get captured. Be prepared to fight."

Little Claws bared his teeth. It wasn't quite a convincing display.

"He's got a harpoon gun," Esquire said. "If the man in the white fur hat picks that up, we stop fighting and give ourselves over, okay? Better to have you stuck in a cage, if it means you're still alive."

Little Claws shook his head. "No, it's not better. I'm

getting back to my mom no matter what, even if I die trying."

"Hello there, animals! Aren't you lucky that I'm here to rescue you?" the man in the white fur hat called.

"Definitely not the way I'd frame it," Esquire muttered.

"I was impressed by your kite, my magical talking fox," the man continued shouting. "It's so unfortunate that it fell apart."

Esquire tried not to react, but she couldn't help it; one of her ears cocked.

"The seams ought to have held," the man said, tapping his lips. "But they didn't. How very odd!"

Esquire couldn't stop herself. She started jumping up and down on the floe, claws sending up sprays of salty ice. "You sabotaged my glider! How dare you!"

"And now, because your little kite fell apart, you're mine," the man said, a wicked smile playing on his lips. "Isn't it marvelous, the way life works?"

"Yes," Esquire muttered as she made some vain attempts to paddle. "It's marvelous."

They were only about forty feet from shore now. The man readied his net, holding it back and off to the side, like he was about to launch a discus. Esquire could imagine the weighted edges of the net flying toward them—

—and suddenly they were! The net's ropes spun across the stretch of sea. Esquire rose on her back legs, in case she could catch the net and somehow cast it away from the floe.

The man in the white fur hat knew what he was doing. It was a direct hit. The weighted edges of the net sank into the sea around the floe, dropping its lattice of rope over Esquire and the cub, pinning them fast against the surface of the ice.

She pushed ferociously against the net, and the cub snarled and bit, but the strands were too thick to bite through. They were trapped.

The scrawny cub kept struggling. Once it was clear

that escape was impossible, Esquire laid a paw on his back. "Save your energy. He'll have to transfer us from the floe to the truck. That's when we'll have our next chance."

But she didn't believe her own words. The man in the white fur hat would only have to pull the lead line, and the net would close tight. There would be no way to escape it.

Even if they did manage to escape, the harpoon gun would be waiting.

The weighted net pressed Esquire into the surface of the ice, immobilizing her. It took all the strength she could muster just to lift her head. Little Claws groaned in fear as the man with the white fur hat reeled them in, a victorious smile twisting his features.

She'd failed. The Animal Rescue Agency had failed. And this innocent little cub would pay the price.

"BRAGH!"

What a strange noise, coming from the other side of the floe. Little Claws glanced around in confusion, but Esquire couldn't summon the energy to turn her head to look at what had caught his attention.

"That must be the sound of failure," she explained.

"The cold got to your brain," Little Claws said. "That's not the sound of failure—it's the sound of a walrus!"

With great difficulty, Esquire managed to turn her head.

What. In. The. World?

It *was* a walrus, the very same ungrateful walrus that Esquire had rescued from the warehouse. Only maybe he was grateful after all, as he was now coursing through the waves toward them. This sudden appearance of a sea monster, with his giant body and thick white-yellow tusks, would have been surprising enough without the additional creature on top of him.

A very wet and bedraggled chicken. Was riding a walrus. A rooster in a tea-cozy coat.

Esquire's mouth hung open. *"Mr. Pepper?"*

"The one and only!" he cock-a-doodled. He might have said something more, but the words were lost when a spray of cold seawater struck him in the face.

The walrus had just his head above the surface, and it was on that head that Mr. Pepper was perched, directing the great beast onward.

"*Mr. Pepper?*" Esquire repeated. Finally, her brain was able to summon more words. "What are you *doing*?"

"I'm rescuing you! What does it look like I'm doing, you numbskull of a fox?"

"Thank you?" Esquire managed.

The man in the white fur hat was yelling curses, but Esquire couldn't make out the words. She was too distracted by the marvelously absurd sight in front of her. The walrus made fast progress through the waves for a creature so bulky, slicing through the icy swells—which unfortunately meant that Mr. Pepper was getting more and more drenched.

Esquire heard a thud and a twang from behind her, and then a dark shape zoomed into view. The man had released the harpoon gun.

Before Esquire could shout a warning, the spear slammed into the ocean, sending up a sharp line of spray. Mr. Pepper squawked in alarm—it had barely missed him and the walrus.

Little Claws bellowed in panic. A curse and then mechanical sounds came from the man in the white fur hat. "Hurry, he's reloading!" Esquire cried.

"Of course we're hurrying!" Mr. Pepper clucked.

Esquire wondered what Mr. Pepper and the walrus planned to do. She was about to find out—they'd reached the floe. The walrus reared back, his wicked tusks gleaming in the morning light.

He was going to attack them? That was the big plan?

"Hold on tight!" Mr. Pepper cried. With that, the walrus did bring his tusks crashing down—but not onto Esquire and the cub. Mr. Pepper flapped his wings to stay on top of the walrus's head while his tusks smashed through the ice floe.

As the floe slanted alarmingly into the ocean, Esquire was suddenly thankful for the net, the only thing keeping her from tumbling into the freezing sea. She heard ice crunching as Little Claws's hind paws desperately tried to dig in. "Hold on to the ropes!" Esquire called.

Waves of cold seawater drenched Esquire's fur as the floe righted itself. She wiped her stinging eyes to see the walrus disengaging from the ice floe—and swimming away! "Wait, what did that accomplish?" she called after Mr. Pepper.

All the while, she could hear the cocking sound as the man in the white fur hat prepared to fire the harpoon gun again.

Her vision was still impeded by the net, so Esquire only barely saw another object fly into view. For a second she worried that another harpoon was on its way—but this object came from the direction of Mr. Pepper.

It was a rope, on the floe for now but rapidly slipping into the sea.

"Through the holes, through the holes!" Mr. Pepper cock-a-doodled.

Esquire lifted her head against the weight of the net and saw that, sure enough, the walrus's tusks had made two holes in the ice, as neat as in a piece of notebook paper. One end of the rope was tied around the walrus's neck, and Mr. Pepper had thrown the other to Esquire.

Little Claws groaned in fear. "He's almost ready to fire again. Hurry!"

Paws shaking, Esquire jammed the end of the rope into one hole and out the other. It was like threading a needle, which meant Mr. Pepper would have been better suited to this. He was the one who did all the darning and embroidery in their household. Still, Esquire managed to get the rope through.

"Now hurl it back!" Mr. Pepper called.

"I know, I know, no one can accuse foxes of being idiots," Esquire grumbled as she darted a paw into frigid seawater to grasp the rope. The walrus was wasting no time—already he was heading back out to open sea, giving Esquire a prime view of Mr. Pepper's iced-over feather-duster butt as the pair departed. She managed to grasp the end of the rope, tug it through, and then tie it, the movements getting a bit wild at the end because of her frozen paws.

"Ready to go!" she called.

"So am I!" came the cruel voice of the man in the white fur hat, just as the rescue rope went tight and began to tug the ice floe along.

The awful twang of the harpoon sounded again, and Esquire braced herself, waiting to feel it impale her to the floe. She scrunched her eyes shut, expecting death. But it hadn't come for her. She opened her eyes to a horrible sight.

Little Claws was curled in a ball on the ice, impossibly small. The harpoon stood straight up, right in the middle of the cub's unmoving form.

CHAPTER

"Little Claws!" Esquire cried, struggling to reach the stricken cub. But the net still pressed her fast to the floe.

The harpoon was stark against the ice. The world became a chaos of frantic whites and grays—the cub, the man in the white fur hat receding, the bright ice and the dark sea. It was like there was no color in anything anymore.

Wait. There was no red on the ice. "Little Claws, can you hear me?" Esquire called.

"No, I can't! The harpoon hit me! I'm dead!" Little Claws cried.

"Not overly dead, from the sound of it," Esquire said.

Little Claws lifted his head against the net, then sat up on his forepaws, like a sphinx. "You're right. I'm not dead!"

"Very nearly were," Esquire said. "Look at that harpoon."

"What harpoon—oh!" Little Claws whipped his head around, trying to find the weapon, in the process banging his sensitive nose right against it. The harpoon had struck the ice right between his rib and leg. An inch in one direction or another and it would have skewered him to the ice.

"You're a lucky little cub, you know that?" Esquire said, tears in her eyes.

Little Claws nodded, eyes wide.

Esquire looked for the man in the white fur hat, and had the pleasure of locating him at the very moment he realized that the polar bear cub had survived the harpoon. He ripped the hat from his head, hurled it to the ground, and stomped on it.

They were far enough away from shore now that the man wouldn't have another chance to attack. They were safe.

"Thank you, Mr. Pepper!" Esquire called.

Mr. Pepper didn't respond—he must be too focused on directing the walrus. He'd taken extra rope and tied himself to the walrus's short neck, so he didn't fall into the sea. Very practical of him.

"Thank you, walrus!" Esquire called.

The walrus grunted in response.

"Thank *you*, Esquire Fox," Little Claws added.

"The Animal Rescue Agency, at your service," Esquire said as she knotted her wet scarf tighter around her neck. The words sounded a little more dignified this time around.

"Do you think we could break through this net somehow?" Little Claws asked.

Esquire shifted as best she could to see him better. "I agree, it's not the most comfortable thing to have every single joint smooshed onto a giant hunk of ice. But even if we could get this net loose, it wouldn't be a good idea yet. It's the only thing keeping us from falling into the sea. Besides, the walrus has us going at a good clip. We have just a short bay to cross until we're in your home territory."

"Will my mother be there?" Little Claws asked.

Esquire stared deep into the cub's dark eyes and smiled. "Of course she will be."

Those dark eyes went watery, then dropped big tears to the ice. "Oh my gosh. I can't wait! I have so much to tell her."

"And then back to full-time snowball fighting," Esquire said, trying to stretch her legs along the ice so that her muscles would uncramp. But the surface was too cold; as soon as she got one muscle unwound, another seized tight. The patience she'd displayed for Little Claws had been a bit of a show. "How much longer will it be?" she called to Mr. Pepper.

Still no answer from the rooster. He might have been squawking something or other, but Esquire couldn't hear it over the sound of the waves.

"I'll never throw a snowball at my mom again," Little Claws vowed.

"Ha. I give that resolution a few hours," Esquire said, tucking her shivering legs as tight as she could, to store up whatever scraps of heat still remained in her body.

She and the polar bear cub entered a trancelike state, shivering and suffering but free. They listened to the waves lapping against the floe, stared up into the gray sky with its dim sunshine. All the while the town of Utqiagvik—and the man in the white fur hat—faded farther and farther from view.

"How's it going up there, Mr. Pepper?" Esquire called.

There was still no answer. Why would he be so silent now? Dread began to dig at the corners of Esquire's thoughts, slipped its cold fingers in no matter where she tried to put her mind.

She couldn't tell how long she stayed that way, pinned to an ice floe on the cold sea, worrying about Mr. Pepper, bracing herself for each wave of cold water that broke over her. The only sounds were the calls of the hardy arctic birds above, the spray of the sea, and the snorting of the walrus as he muscled them through the breakers.

Finally, the rope groaned as it went taut, then the floe lurched to a stop. Ice crunched as the walrus pulled himself onto shore. "Okay, all off now!" he called.

"We would if we could!" Esquire said, still pinned to the ice.

"Oh, right," the walrus said, then set to work cutting the net, making short work of it by pulling and sawing with his tusks.

As soon as she could, Esquire got to four paws—and promptly tumbled to her chin. There wasn't any feeling in her limbs.

The floe rocked as Little Claws dragged himself onto solid ground. Esquire shut her eyes, girding herself. If she didn't move, she would die, and she was *not* going to die on some hunk of ice in the Arctic. She wrapped her wet jacket around herself, then staggered to all fours, managing to stay upright this time. Gathering up as much dignity as she could, she gave her body a good shake, picked her way out of the remnants of the net, and hauled herself onto shore.

Little Claws was on the snowy ground, skinny limbs out akimbo as he sniffed the air. He was trying to see if his mother was nearby, no doubt. The walrus sat up, catching his breath, tusks glimmering in the dim light of midday. Mr. Pepper was still lashed to the back of his neck. Esquire could just make out the feathers of his backside.

"Are you stuck up there, Mr. Pepper?" Esquire called. The rooster didn't move. "Mr. Pepper?"

While Esquire lurched her way to the walrus, the beast watched her with liquid, searching eyes. "Your chicken friend got blasted with a lot of cold seawater," he said.

"What are you trying to say?" Esquire asked. She was already hard at work untying the ropes fastening

Mr. Pepper. Her frozen paws had a hard go of it, and her eyes unexpectedly welled with tears as she tore at the frozen knots.

Mr. Pepper's feathers were covered in crystals. Frozen solid.

Finally, Esquire got the ropes undone and pulled Mr. Pepper from the walrus. Icicles tinkled to the ground as she wrenched the rooster free.

"Mr. Pepper?" Esquire said, more crystals spraying as she ran her paws over the stiff feathers on his chest. His eyes were shut tight, his beak stuck open in mid-caw. "Mr. Pepper!"

He was still, still, still. Esquire held his unmoving body to her chest and cried.

CHAPTER

Esquire crumpled right where she stood, Mr. Pepper tight in her embrace. She was dimly aware of the walrus staring mournfully at her, and of Little Claws mewling nearby, but all her attention was on the rooster cradled in her forelegs, frozen within his tea cozy. Not a coat. A tea cozy.

How could Esquire have let Mr. Pepper come to the Arctic?

Unaware of the chill in her own body now, Esquire buried her nose in Mr. Pepper's feathers. Because her nose was so cold, she couldn't detect his familiar smell, the lemon oil scent he always had from polishing the furniture. They'd extended themselves too much, gone too far from home, hadn't been prepared enough. Esquire's plan had been too reckless, and Mr. Pepper had paid the ultimate price.

She sensed commotion nearby, heard Little Claws shout, felt the icy ground vibrate as he jumped up and down. "Have some respect!" Esquire snapped, wiping tears from her eyes.

But the commotion didn't die down. When Esquire finally looked over, her jaw dropped open.

Racing toward her was the most massive predator she'd ever seen. The bear was a muscular tower of white fur, teeth bared and claws outstretched as she barreled in Esquire's direction. The walrus brayed in fear, lumbering into the sea.

Esquire's first thought was that she was about to die. Her second? That at least then she'd be with Mr. Pepper.

Desperate beyond all fear, she whirled on the monstrous bear that had come to eat her up. She'd go down fighting.

Little Claws kept jumping up and down. He must have been thrilled that his mom had finally arrived to help him eat this orange stranger and her frozen chicken entrée. Esquire ripped off her jacket and went full fox, snarling and snapping at them, beyond words.

No dignity, no natty outfit, all vixen.

"Get out of the way!" Little Claws screamed.

"You can't have him!" Esquire screamed back, whirling with Mr. Pepper clutched to her chest. "Getting eaten by a polar bear is just what we thought would happen to Mr. Pepper if he came here, but he came anyway, to help me, and now look!" She shrieked at the sky, a feral and wordless sound. "Even if he's dead now, I won't let you eat him, or me! He's—" her voice broke off in a sob. "He's coming home."

"Esquire Fox! Please get out of the way!" Little Claws repeated.

Esquire's deep sorrow heated into anger instead. Holding Mr. Pepper's unmoving form under one foreleg, like a football, Esquire wagged her other paw at Little Claws. "Did you not listen to the speech I just made?"

The giant polar bear wasn't slowing down. In a matter of seconds, it would be upon her.

"My mom has the warmest fur ever!" Little Claws said, leaping up and down.

"What's that got to do with anything?" Esquire retorted. Her voice trailed off. "Oh! Do you really think . . . ?"

"Get out of the way!" Little Claws repeated.

Esquire couldn't let go of Mr. Pepper. She held him out to the giant sprinting polar bear, tears streaming down her face. "Please help—"

Then the great beast was upon her. Big Claws bowled Esquire right over, tackling her and sending them both rolling, almost right into the sea. Esquire tumbled through snow and ice, losing track of Mr. Pepper, seeing him aloft and flying through the air like a badminton birdie. By the time she staggered to her paws, she saw that Mr. Pepper was deep in Big Claws's clutches.

This massive killer, one of the most ferocious predators in the natural world, was holding Mr. Pepper like an infant.

It was too hard to imagine that this polar bear could be saving her friend instead of eating him. Esquire couldn't stop herself from snarling and lunging toward the giant carnivore. "It's okay!" the bear called to Esquire, holding up a paw to stop her. "I'm trying to help!"

Esquire made herself stop. She stared, open-jawed and heart racing, as the big polar bear sat on the ice, tucking Mr. Pepper deep into her belly fur. She rocked him like a baby.

"Is that going to work?" Esquire asked.

"Getting snuggled by Mom is the best feeling *ever*," Little Claws said as he bounded over. "You should try it after that chicken's done!"

"Oh, I don't know about that," Esquire said. She rubbed her frozen paws. Actually, it did look pretty great. It was hard to imagine anything snugglier than a polar bear's belly.

Mr. Pepper's feathers were thawing, beading with condensation. It remained to be seen, though, if the rest of him would stay a corpse or turn back into a living rooster. Esquire's tears crystallized into ice droplets before they could drip off her snout.

"My name is Big Claws. Thank you for everything you've done," the polar bear said. "I sent out that distress call, and I honestly didn't think it could possibly work, but here you are, and you saved my son! I could just—wait, what's this?"

Mr. Pepper's coxcomb was pale, and even his beak seemed to have turned blue around the edges. So Esquire was taken by surprise when Mr. Pepper wheezed.

"Did you hear that?" Esquire cried, reaching out a paw to clutch one of the walrus's flippers. He startled. He'd warily returned from the sea, but was not particularly interested in the fates of chickens and had instead been trying to catch some sun.

Little Claws hopped up and down. "Look, look, that delicious bird is breathing again!"

Big Claws smiled at the wet bundle of feathers in her forelegs. "He's all thawed through. I honestly wasn't sure if he was going to make it. That's one tough chicken."

"You don't know the half of it," Esquire said, somehow rolling her eyes even as she cried tears of joy.

"If he's tough, I guess that means he wouldn't have

tasted too good anyway," Little Claws said, disappointed.

"The eating-Mr.-Pepper comments will end now, thank you," Esquire scolded.

"I was kidding," Little Claws protested, holding up his front paws. "Or at least I was probably kidding!"

Big Claws gave Mr. Pepper to Esquire while she fixed her son with a stern look. Then her face melted with relief. "Come here, my Little Claws," Big Claws said, opening her forelegs.

Little Claws bounded over and disappeared into her embrace. "I was so worried about you, little bear," Big Claws said. "That awful man in the white fur hat. We'll stay even farther north from here on out." She hugged him even tighter. "You've gotten so skinny."

"I am *very* hungry," Little Claws said, nodding.

The walrus gave the polar bears a baleful look, then wiggled his hairy jowls at Esquire. "I know these polar bears feel grateful to us, but they're still polar bears. I'd recommend we get moving."

Esquire nodded. "I'd like to get Mr. Pepper in front of a warm fire as soon as possible."

Big Claws grunted. "You have nothing to worry about from us. But it's true—we've had a hard time finding enough food to eat over the summers, and now we've lost an extra week. Little Claws and I need to start hunting right away. But Esquire, I want you to know that I will always do anything I can to help you. You saved my cub when no one else could. I will forever be in the Animal Rescue Agency's debt."

Esquire stroked Mr. Pepper's feathers. He seemed to be in a deep sleep, clucking as he dreamed. Steam rose from his soaked tea-cozy coat. "Thank you," Esquire said.

"Mom, Mom, I want to join the Animal Rescue Agency!" Little Claws said, wrestling himself out of his mother's forelegs.

"You want to go live in—where are you located again?" Big Claws asked, amused.

"Colorado," Esquire said.

Big Claws tilted her head.

"ArmadilloPikaKingsnakeLoon," Esquire said, sighing.

Big Claws nodded. "So you want to go live in ArmadilloPikaKingsnakeLoon?"

"No," Little Claws said, ears sagging. "I want to live here with you. But I also want to stop bad guys!"

"I could always use more regional agents," Esquire said. "I have a moose in Anchorage, but you could be my first polar agent. Mr. Pepper will be so thrilled that we expanded our network!"

"Polar agent," Little Claws said, trying out the words. "That sounds very important."

"It is," Esquire said. "I'll be much obliged for your service. If you see any sign of the man in the white fur hat, for example, I'd like you to send word as soon as you can."

Little Claws nodded solemnly. "I'll either eat him or send you word. Maybe both."

Esquire shrugged. "Fair enough. That's a very polar bear sort of plan."

"Is there an initiation ceremony or anything cool like that?" Little Claws asked.

"No, it's all official now," Esquire said. "I'll send you tax forms each January."

"What's a tax form?" Little Claws asked.

"Don't worry about it," Esquire said. Jokes were always tricky to pull off across species lines. She turned to the walrus. "So do you think I could snag a ride back to Utqiagvik?"

"You rescued me from life in a cage. I'd take you down to the Bahamas if you wanted."

"Ooh, the Bahamas!" Esquire said, toying with a whisker.

"No," the walrus said.

"But you just said—"

"Get on before I change my mind," he ordered.

Esquire snuggled Mr. Pepper tight into the crook of her elbow and used her free paw to pick up the restraining rope. "We'll get you home soon, Mr. Pepper. I won't complain about your pecking the furniture, not ever again."

The ship's hull thrummed as it chugged through the sea, sending pleasant vibrations up and down Esquire's spine. After she got home from a difficult case, she would sometimes bring in a local Colorado mole massage team to jump up and down on her back to loosen the muscles—but she might not need to hire them this time. The ship was doing the trick.

Freighter was really a marvelous way to travel. Better than husky. Much better than walrus.

It had all been set up by the Utqiagvik rats. They had cousins on every ship that came through town. (Rat family trees make giant complicated knots. Their weddings are always epic affairs.) When Esquire explained her situation—needing to get a near-comatose rooster back to ArmadilloPikaKingsnakeLoon—the rats quickly made the introduction and helped get Mr. Pepper snuggled away into the hold as soon as possible.

So here Esquire was, resting up in a hammock she'd rigged from an empty onion sack (whose smell still made her sneeze every once in a while), lulled by the rumble of the freighter's engines. She'd positioned the hammock by an eyelet in the hull, which meant she could spend the day basking in a ray of sunshine. Filling her lungs with ocean air as she munched on what remained of the mushroom jerky Mr. Pepper had packed for the trip, Esquire flipped through the home decorating magazine she'd pilfered from the drugstore.

In any other circumstances, she might take the opportunity to wander the ship and perhaps rifle through the cargo. Right now, though, she didn't want to leave her hammock. That might disturb Mr. Pepper.

His beak was no longer the disquieting blue gray it had been in the Arctic, and the rooster made faint little snores as he slept. Though her friend was plenty warm now, Esquire still kept her bushy orange tail wrapped snugly around him. She even did her best to preen him, removing any feathers that were obviously sticking out, smoothing the oil at the base of each quill through the entire feather. She knew how upset Mr. Pepper would be if he woke up looking a mess.

That wakeup seemed about to happen. Mr. Pepper's eyes fluttered open to see Esquire's big fox face staring right back. Every feather on the rooster's face went rigid, sticking straight out.

"Hello there," Esquire said, displaying her teeth.

Mr. Pepper squawked and tumbled out of the hammock, cock-a-doodle-doodling his head off as he ran in panicked circles.

"Shh! It's me, you old fool!" Esquire said, hopping to the floor and running after him with open paws. Open paws only meant displaying her sharp claws, though, which made Mr. Pepper squawk even louder.

Mr. Pepper finally remembered himself and shut his beak. "Oh."

Esquire glanced to the hold's hatch, to see if any humans had heard them and were coming to investigate. But apparently the noise of the engines had been enough to cover even Mr. Pepper's squawks.

The rooster's tail feathers went straight up as he strutted around the hold. "What infernal place have you trapped us in now?"

"It's a freighter," Esquire sniffed, "and up until you woke up, I was thinking it was an excellent way to travel."

"Preposterous. Only you would think it was a good idea to entomb ourselves in a hunk of steel in the middle of the sea."

Esquire stifled a smile.

Mr. Pepper was not done. "What was wrong with going back the way we came?"

"You see, Mr. Pepper, you were unconscious. That made it too tricky to travel by husky."

"Unconscious? Me? I beg to differ. I was taking a nap. Quite different."

"Ah. It was a very deep nap."

Mr. Pepper's tail feathers softened. "Thank you for finding us a way back home, Esquire."

"You're welcome. There, Mr. Pepper. That wasn't so hard." Esquire had been trying to find the words to tell Mr. Pepper that his outrage sometimes hurt her feelings a little bit. But maybe he'd realized as much on his own.

"Normally I would trust only myself with preparations like this," Mr. Pepper said, "but it's good to see you're able to make some logistical decisions in a pinch."

"Thank you, Mr. Pepper. I think."

"So. Just how are we getting from the Pacific coast back to the lair?"

Esquire sighed. "I was figuring we'd take it as it goes."

"That's no plan at all! It's a good thing I woke up when I did."

"It certainly is," Esquire said, and meant it. "I don't know what I would have done if you hadn't."

Mr. Pepper pecked at the onion sack. "You've been sleeping in this?"

"Yes," Esquire said, unlatching the valise's brass fasteners and pulling out a smaller sack. "I snagged an empty brussels sprout bag for you."

Mr. Pepper shuddered. All the same, he allowed Esquire to tack it up, giving her frequent instructions as she did. Once his hammock was securely in place, Mr. Pepper hopped right in, coxcomb already drooping as he began to nod off.

"The man in the white fur hat," Mr. Pepper said. "Were you able to put a stop to his operation?"

"We freed all his captives and kept the polar bear cub out of his clutches," Esquire said, "so I consider this a victory. But he's still out there."

She would wait until Mr. Pepper was fully awake to tell him about the moment at the port. As the freighter had been pulling away, Esquire had looked out of the eyelet to see the man in the white fur hat on the dock, staring after the departing ship. Their eyes had locked. She'd been paralyzed for a moment. Once Esquire had recovered herself, she'd scrambled into her hammock. By the time she'd gathered the nerve to look back out, the man had been gone.

"He's probably eager for revenge," Mr. Pepper said. "That's not good. We'll have to add him to our villain wall."

"Yes, I do imagine this isn't the last we'll be seeing of him," Esquire said, straightening her jacket and fluffing her cream-colored scarf around her neck. Even with her thick fur, the onion sack was a little prickly wherever it touched her directly.

"After this nap I'll do the balance sheet for this operation," Mr. Pepper said from somewhere within the brussels sprout sack. "Foxes are not good with ledgers, and I like to make sure we keep exact numbers of what our clients have given us in compensation."

Within her onion sack, Esquire went perfectly rigid.

"Roughly how much did we make, Esquire?" Mr. Pepper asked.

A tingling dread wrapped its fingers around Esquire's ribs.

"Esquire?" Mr. Pepper said, his voice rising dangerously at the end.

"Well, you see, um, I can't really say that I, that I um . . ."

Suddenly Mr. Pepper was out of his sack and hopping up and down, flapping around the hold. "ESQUIRE FOX! How many times have I told you, we can't run a business without billing!"

Esquire let out a heavy sigh. It was going to be a very long trip back home.

To each animal,
the right to live a natural life

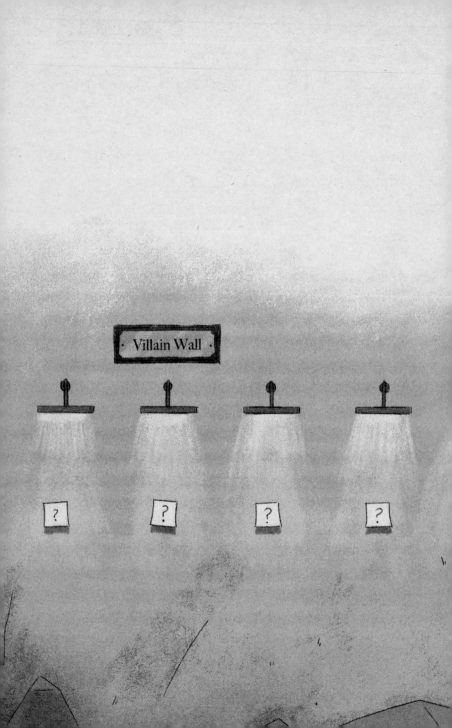

Hello! Esquire Fox here. Mr. Pepper insists that I type up field notes after each mission. To be honest I'd rather just have the adventure and be done with it than sit around hunting for the right keys on this frustrating keyboarddddd. Anyway, it's been two weeks since our time in the Arctic, and I will have an irate rooster on my paws if I don't finally write something about our trip.

Let's see. For starters, you might have noticed that Little Claws was careful to jump on ice to test it after he ventured out of his den. This is because the Arctic is warming, and each year there is less ice left. Even "multiyear ice," or ice that hasn't melted for centuries, is disappearing under higher temperatures. Polar bears have to be careful where they walk, if they don't want to be unexpectedly thrust into the sea.

The problem goes deeper than that, though! Faster ice melt also means the polar bears have less time to eat seals in the spring and fatten up before the summer, when food is most scarce. It also interferes with the growth of algae on the ice. Little Claws and Big Claws wouldn't deign to eat algae themselves, but plankton do—then fish eat the plankton, and seals eat the fish. When the food chain gets disrupted, the bears start to starve.

The man in the white fur hat was the human who caused all the trouble for Little Claws and Big Claws. The general threat to polar bears is also caused by humans. It might not be as literal as a hunter chasing down a cub, but it's just as deadly. There is overwhelming scientific consensus that the release of greenhouse gases from human activity is the primary cause of the rise in temperatures that threatens the existence of the polar bears.

Humans are also the animal world's greatest hope for change, though! Any person who wants to help can join the global fight to stop climate change. For starters, you could check out "What are the most important things kids can do to prevent global warming?" on the American Museum of Natural History's website.

Want to read more? Here are some reputable sources, the same ones I used to gather the information for these field notes:

"Arctic sea ice has been in decline for decades,"
National Snow & Ice Data Center,
www.NSIDC.org

"The surprising reason polar bears
need sea ice to survive,"
National Geographic,
www.nationalgeographic.com

"The Causes of Climate Change,"
National Aeronautics and Space Administration,
www.climate.nasa.gov

That's all for now! I'm off to go put my paws up and listen to my favorite jazz record.

Yours truly,

Esquire Fox

FROM THE KITCHEN OF MR. PEPPER:

MUSHROOM JERKY

If you are a child, kid, foal, colt, hatchling, larva, or fry, you must get an adult's help to make this. Mr. Pepper doesn't want you to burn or slice yourself.

INGREDIENTS:
• 8 ounces of mushrooms (Shiitake will make for the meatiest jerky possible. Esquire has been known, however, to equally enjoy ordinary white mushrooms.)
• Olive oil
• Salt and pepper

STEPS:
• Heat oven to 425°F.
• To clean the mushrooms, gently rub them with a moist cloth or paper towel. Don't get them fully wet, or your jerky will come out soggy.
• If you are using shiitake mushrooms, remove the woody stem. (Save this to make a mushroom tea

over a campfire when you and Esquire need to relax after a long day's mission.) If you are using standard white mushrooms, the stem can remain.

• Have an adult help slice your mushrooms. One-half-an-inch thickness is a good rule of claw. Slice them thinner to have something closer to a chip; thicker will make for chewier jerky.

• Place the mushroom slices on a cookie sheet. Drizzle them with plenty of olive oil and toss until they're coated. (This is easier if you have hands than if you have chicken feet, though the oil is a terrific moisturizer for one's scaly skin.)

• Arrange slices in a single layer and bake until they are deep golden brown, or about 25 minutes. Don't let them blacken.

• Remove from oven and sprinkle with plenty of salt and pepper. Let them cool for at least 10 minutes before eating. (Do not allow Esquire into the kitchen during this time!)

(Thank you to human chef Kate Merker
for her assistance with this recipe.)

ACKNOWLEDGMENTS

I'm very grateful to Esquire and Mr. Pepper for offering a measly human like me some space to add a few words of thanks.

First of all, hats off to my agent, Richard Pine, and my editor, Ben Rosenthal, for so expertly ushering this book series to the page. The whole team at Katherine Tegen Books has been amazing. Extra thanks to Jenny Moles for her top-notch copyediting. Zack Clark and Eric Zahler were also foundational in shaping *The Animal Rescue Agency* in its earliest stages.

This book owes a ton to its sharp kid readers: thanks to Jules, Hazel, Charlie, and Simon (as well as their parents Danielle, Kate, Justin, and Kristin). Kate Merker, an extra shout-out for coming up with that mushroom jerky—it truly is delicious!

I'm grateful to my fellow students and colleagues in the New York University Animal Studies program, for helping continue to broaden my thinking about what bonds humans and nonhumans.

As always, thanks to my writer friends who read manuscripts and lend a friendly ear: Daphne Benedis-Grab, Donna Freitas, Marie Rutkoski, Marianna Baer, Jill Santopolo, Anne Heltzel, Anna Godbersen, and my mother, Barbara Schrefer.

Esquire needs the computer back. I'm signing off until the next case file arrives—here's hoping it's for someplace warm! —E.S.

TURN THE PAGE FOR A SNEAK PEEK AT THE
ANIMAL RESCUE AGENCY'S
NEXT ADVENTURE!

J ewel the pangolin had been having the most wonderful dream. She'd been lost in the trees, surrounded
by so many shades of green, so many humming insects
and chirping frogs. Her sharp front claws had broken
open a crumbly log, and inside were fat ants. Slurp,
slurp, slurp with her long tongue, and down they went.

It turned out she'd been slurping her pillow. When
she opened her eyes, she saw the silk was covered in goo
from her sticky saliva. How unclassy. Jewel delicately
turned the pillow over. There, no one would notice.

She pressed her claws over her eyes and tried to live
inside the dream for a few more minutes. She didn't

remember ever visiting a place like that, but the last few nights she'd dreamed of the same jungle. So many leaves (and delicious ants!) in one place. Where had this fantasy land come from? As far as she could remember, her life had been only private jets and fancy hotels.

Jewel looked around to see if anyone had spotted her drooling, but the resort hotel room was empty. How strange. Her beloved owner—Dizzy Dillinger, the biggest human pop star in the world—wasn't there. His other exotic pets, Butch the wildcat and Arabella the monkey, weren't there. Neither was Jewel's brother, Beatle.

Where *was* everyone?

Then Jewel looked out of the villa's window and saw that the sun, which she thought really ought to be up at the top of the sky, was closer to the horizon, turning the sea orange.

She was late!

On instinct Jewel rolled into a tight ball, her scales sticking out everywhere. But that was no help—that strategy was for predators! Not that her dear Dizzy would ever let her get near any of those. Jewel unrolled herself, whiskers trembling, then scampered off the silk pillow and out the door. "You're a star," she scolded herself. "You better act like it."

She got her nerves under control and stepped haughtily down the corridor. Dizzy Dillinger always insisted that his pets be allowed to freely roam whatever resort he was staying in. The hallway was all a blur—everything was always a blur to Jewel, actually, with her weak pangolin eyes—but it was full of smells that gave a lot of information to her sensitive nose. She could detect Caribbean seawater on the other side of the billowing curtains, the fragrance of the individual ants marching through the walls, and the scent of humans all around. That was Dizzy's friends and road crew, preparing for his big concert that weekend.

She easily tracked her brother's fragrance, following it through the hallways, calmly stepping between human legs all the while. One particularly awkward-looking human tried to pet her. (Ew! No way!) Finally she climbed a staircase bannister to get to Beatle's dressing room.

Before she went in, she double-checked that there was no more drool crusted on the tip of her nose. Her brother teased her whenever she looked less than perfect.

Beatle's dressing room was what a human would have called a cosmetics trunk, but Dizzy's pets knew it was much more than that. Inside was a paradise of colors. One side was covered top to bottom in bottles of nail polish, a rainbow of blueberries and lemons and plums. Beatle had a strawberry-red bottle in one claw and was delicately applying the color to the smallest scales at the tip of his tail.

The polish was a big reason for Beatle's fame in the animal world. He spent hours painting himself before each concert or even a dress rehearsal, like tonight. It was an amazing effect, which was why his concerts drew even bigger crowds than Dizzy's. (To be fair, anytime roaches and rabbits are invited to an event, the attendance numbers get very big very quickly.)

"You're late, sister," Beatle snapped. "My Indigo Intensity scales are still going to be wet during the rehearsal."

"I'm sorry, Beatle!" Jewel said, casting her eyes to the black velvet at the bottom of the trunk. "I was having that dream again, the one with all the trees and the frogs and the bugs—"

"Hurry up," Beatle interrupted. "The bottle's over there."

"I thought you loved this part of the day," Jewel grumbled. Her brother was the only creature in her life that dared to order her around. She picked up the polish in her front claws, her sensitive nose wrinkling at its harsh scent. Beatle liked to do most of his rainbow himself, but he couldn't reach the scales behind his neck. Those were his sister's responsibility.

She held her breath as she stroked Indigo Intensity between her brother's shoulders. "It looks just as beautiful as always," she said.

In the good old days, her brother would have sighed and asked her to fetch a mirror so he could admire the color, and they would have oohed and aahed for a while. But lately he'd become so irritable. "Don't forget, it's turn-turn-shuffle during the new chorus, not turn-shuffle-turn," he said.

"Yep, don't worry, I've got it," Jewel said. "You forget you're talking to the best backup dancer in the whole animal kingdom. Now stop wiggling, or you're going to smear Indigo Intensity all over your Cornflower Morning."

"Sorry, sis," Beatle said. "It's just that everyone's expecting a perfect show from me. These animals are coming from so far away. It's a lot of pressure."

"You and Dizzy are definitely two of a kind," Jewel

said, shaking her head. "Your shows are always perfect, but you always worry yourself miserable about them."

Beatle let out a long sigh. Jewel almost asked him to explain what was on his mind, but then Beatle briskly shivered his scales and shook a bottle of see-through polish. "I set some Crystal Clear aside for you."

"That's okay, I'm just the backup dancer, I don't need any polish for the rehearsal. *You're* the star."

Beatle smiled, clearly feeling a little better. This was a routine that they did before every performance, where she worked up his confidence. "I wish we didn't have to keep our shows hidden from humans like Dizzy," Beatle said, carefully slotting the nail polish into the rack. "I bet he'd be proud of us."

"No one will be proud of you if you're late to your own dress rehearsal. Come on!" Jewel said. She climbed out of the cosmetics trunk, crawled up some nearby curtains, and dropped out an open window.

Beatle plopped to the sandy ground beside her, shaking his claws. "I just put on this Creamsicle Orange, and it's already getting covered in sand. That stuff is everywhere around here."

"I know, it's a tragedy," Jewel said. "Poor you, suffering on a private island in the Bahamas."

"If the animals see anything imperfect, they'll be

disappointed," Beatle sniffed. "Let's try to find me disposable booties to wear before the actual concert, so I don't look like a clod of sand out there."

Dizzy Dillinger was hosting a weeklong party on his island, with fancy humans sailing in on their yachts for his concert on the last evening. As usual, Beatle would copy Dizzy's schedule to the minute—with his own animal fans traveling in from all over the world. (Though they would be arriving by sea turtle and albatross instead of by yacht and private plane.)

As a backup dancer, Jewel knew that she wasn't feeling nearly the pressure that her brother was. "They're all here for your voice, not your Creamsicle Orange polish," she said. "Now, let's get a move on. The crew is waiting."

"What even is a Creamsicle?" Beatle asked.

"I have no idea," Jewel said. "Some human thing." She filled her nose with the scents of the outdoors. Most animals flocked to the area for the black-sand beaches and the baby-blue water, but for Jewel the beauties of the Caribbean were all the wonderful smells. Here the air was full of salt and pine, way better than the stale, dried-out odors of their pet suite.

The pangolin brother and sister picked their way along the sand and scrub, toward the rocky plateau.

There, the iguana roadies were checking the stage. They'd positioned the structure (actually a TV stand borrowed from a hotel room) on a rocky plateau overlooking the sea. For safety they were tying it to the rocks, leaving a crawl space beneath. The sun would set right behind Beatle as he gave his show, glinting off his multicolored scales and the waves beyond.

Butch the wildcat was sitting where the animal audience would be for the actual concert, cleaning his glossy fur while he pretended not to watch the hutias rigging lights up in the bushes. The rodents were positioning and repositioning LEDs from the hotel's freebie key chains until they converged on the middle of the stage. Butch barely looked Beatle and Jewel's way before returning to licking the striped fur between his thick claws. "I see you two have finally decided to join us."

"Maybe I was just building dramatic tension," Beatle sniffed.

"Talent on the set!" called a voice from a nearby palm tree. It was Arabella the monkey, the third of Dizzy Dillinger's exotic pets—and the show's director. "My whole family's on their way from Costa Rica to see the concert, you know that? Better be good! Don't embarrass me, okay?" She had something in her hand, which she bit into with gusto. She scowled and let it drop to the ground. "I thought that was a fig. It was definitely not a fig." She took out an old birthday hat, which she'd snipped the end off to make a monkey-sized megaphone. "Places, everyone! Let's get ready to make art!"

Beatle climbed to the center of the stage, stood up on his hind legs, and fanned his painted claws in front of his face. "How do I look?"

"Gorgeous as always," Jewel said as she took up her position at the rear. She noticed a circular cut in the stage, right around where Beatle was standing. "What's that?" she called.

"Arabella added an effect," Butch growled. "A platform is going to rise up in the middle of the first number. It's a little overdramatic if you ask me."

"Music! Start the music!" Arabella shrieked from the palms. "We can't have a show without music!"

One of the hutias tried to press the button on the portable speaker. Nothing happened. It tried leaping on it. Still nothing. Hutias don't have a lot of muscle.

Butch sighed. "I guess I have to do everything. As usual." The hutia scampered away as Butch padded over to the speaker and pressed a button. An electronic dance beat thudded out. "That sounds awful," Butch yelled over the noise. "Maybe you'll reconsider having a live band."

That "live band," of course, used to be Butch himself. He would pluck a harp and sing and bang a drum with his tail, all at the same time. It was . . . impressive. As in it made an impression. Of being painful to the ears. Now that Beatle had switched to recorded music, Butch's only responsibility was keeping guard.

"Three measures of lead-in!" Arabella called. "Places, pangolins. Five, six, seven, eight!"

Jewel's role was easy. She shuffled back and forth to the tempo of the electronica, shaking her hips and making her tail wave like a ribbon. Occasionally she sang "ooh, ooh."

Her brother, though, really was breathtaking. His rainbow of nail polish reflected the light from the setting sun, making a sherbet smear of colors.

And that was before he opened his mouth to sing!

The closest sound to a pangolin's voice is wind chimes. The moment Beatle began to sing his number one hit, "Every Scale is Major," all the animals within earshot went still. Even Butch's tail relaxed, and his ears went back.

Jewel's brother really was talented. She had been

trying to convince him for years that his voice was enough; he didn't need to add rainbow scales and an electronic beat. But he always wanted to be improving, so he wouldn't let everyone down.

This time, though, she found she wasn't able to concentrate on her brother's performance. The stage wobbled as she crossed back and forth. Just a little bit of tilt, but any wobble was too much when you were on top of a cliff. "Excuse me," she called to the nearest iguana roadie, "did you already test the stage?"

"What?" the iguana called back, cupping a claw behind his scaly ear. "I can't hear you!"

The reason he couldn't hear Jewel was that the music had reached its thundering climax. The circle beneath Beatle began to rumble. Instead of lifting, like Arabella had said it would, it began to sink!

"Stop the music!" Jewel shrieked.

The music continued to blare on as the platform sank even more.

As the trapdoor dropped beneath the stage, Beatle locked eyes with his sister. "Help me, Jewel!" he called.

She reached out for him. It felt like time had slowed, that she'd never reach her brother. As she got near, she saw his midsection disappear, and then his neck. For a moment her brother's head was there, and then it was . . . gone!

Jewel reached the edge of the trapdoor and peered down below. There was a giant gap in the rock, a crevasse leading far down into the earth. Her brother had disappeared down it. Completely vanished. "Beatle!" she cried.

She listened for a response but couldn't hear anything over the ruckus. "Cut the music!" she cried.

Butch turned off the electronica, and the evening air again filled with the chirping of the island cicadas. "Beatle?" Jewel tried again.

"I'm trapped down here!" came his voice. It was quiet, almost impossible to hear. He was very far away.

Arabella scampered to the edge and peered in, her eyes wide with astonishment. "You can hear him, with your super pangolin hearing?" she asked Jewel.

Jewel nodded. "He's way, way down this hole."

The rest of the animals approached in shocked silence. The iguana and hutia roadies, Arabella and Butch, every one of them struck dumb by what had happened.

How could the lift, which was supposed to send Beatle up into the air, have dropped him into this crevasse instead? "Beatle!" Jewel cried again.

She heard a soft scramble from far below, a yelp from Beatle, and then nothing. He must have fallen even deeper in.

Jewel's mind spun. In the corner of her brain, a thought was already forming.

They had to get Beatle out before he starved, or before the whole thing caved in. But how to manage that, when he was deep down a hole?

She was in over her head.

She needed help.

And when an animal truly needed help, there was only one place to turn.

The Animal Rescue Agency.